"MY WIFE, my own wife—and I don't even know where she is sleeping . . . or if she is sleeping alone . . ."

—this was Jud's one obsessing thought as he catapulted aloft in the hottest jet ever built . . .

The X-14A was hardly off the engineers' drawing boards. It was designed to reach new altitudes and a speed of Mach 3 (three times faster than the speed of sound). It held the hopes and dreams of its builders—of a nation . . .

But it also carried a pilot who couldn't keep his mind on the controls—and off a woman!

JET
PILOT

WILDSIDE PRESS

Gratefully dedicated to Dan Darnell, J. O. Roberts, J. Ray Donahue, Ray Morris, Bob Baker, Bob Hoover and Bud Poage, test pilots at North American Aviation, Inc., Los Angeles, and First Lieutenant Robert F. Hazeleaf, USAF.

And with utmost respect to George Welch, killed testing the F-100, and Joe Lynch, killed testing the F-86.

Chapter One

SINCE HE usually kept a light touch on the stick, he was surprised to find himself overcontrolling slightly as he began his initial approach. The feeling passed quickly, however, as he busied himself with the numerous details of getting the slim fighter-bomber back to the runway.

When he was 1500 feet up and slowing to 300 knots, he got the speed brakes out and called the L.A. tower. His eyes skimmed over the dozens of instruments and gauges and for just a second he thought about Chally and the way those big glossy eyes of hers had shone that night she'd tasted her first Martini. Or at least she'd said it was her first.

He made sure the hydraulic pressures were normal and that the emergency fuel switch was off and then he made his pitch-out, feeling a little half-G tug in his belly as the airplane banked cleanly over the runway.

A yellow bulldozer was nosing into a mound of dirt on the port side of the strip and Judson made a mental note to keep over on the far right.

At 220 knots he dropped his flaps. At 185 he dropped his wheels and the afternoon sunlight gleamed brightly along the wing as he banked again and radioed the tower that his gear was green and his pressure was up. Gradually the nose dropped and when he was sure of his position over the runway he chopped the throttle, reducing the roar of the jet to a scream and then a moan.

He hit the asphalt fast, touching the rear two wheels first and from the edge of his eye seeing the long silver row of brakes and let the engine idle for a couple of minutes to stabil-
Chally had laughed that same night when he'd told her the story about Dunc's pet white mouse, throwing her head back so the perfect long line of her throat showed. It was really quite remarkable how he could recall all those little things

5

about her, like the aqua ribbon she tucked over her ear and the way those gray slacks fitted her trim little waist.

He let the airplane speed nearly a half a mile before he allowed the nose wheel to touch and then he began toeing the brakes with a gentle intermittent pressure. After he'd slowed sufficiently, he turned her and taxied off the runway to the parking area south of the engineering testing hangar.

The crewmen waved him into a position between two other Lancers parked on the line and then he pulled on the parking brakes and let the engine idle for a couple of minutes to stabilize the temperatures. As he sat there, sweat running down his ribs, he suddenly felt very tired—as if he'd been flying all day instead of for half an hour. He pulled the throttle sharply to off, the engine died and he was grateful for the reduced pressure against his eardrums.

He disconnected the G-suit and oxygen hoses, removed his helmet and briefly massaged his cheeks and the back of his neck before checking off the myriad number of electrical and mechanical controls.

Eddie, one of the crew chiefs, set up a ladder and came up to the cockpit as Judson slid the plastic canopy back.

"Pretty good run?" Eddie asked.

"So, so," said Judson.

Eddie handed him the safety pins, with their long red warning flags, and Judson methodically installed them in the ejection seat and canopy systems.

Then, carrying his white helmet in one gloved hand, he got out of the cockpit and descended the ladder. As he signed the maintenance sheet for Eddie he felt a little nausea in his belly and he wondered if he were getting a touch of the flu that was going around the plant. On the other hand it might just be that hamburger and second bottle of beer he'd had over at Ditman's.

"I happened to look up when you done those Cuban Eights," said Eddie. "Man, they were beautiful."

Judson handed Eddie back his pencil. "They felt a little ragged."

"Hell, they didn't look ragged," said Eddie. "Even bitchy-drawers Bixler couldn't do 'em that clean."

Judson shrugged, skirted the scarlet-enameled testing boom on the wing tip and started walking toward the hangar. The

6

chute with its bail-out bottle felt heavy and sweaty where it pressed against his back and he slipped out of the shoulder harness so he could carry the rig in his right hand.

Obdorsk, holding a bundle of notebooks and reports, was waiting for him when he got to the base of the test flight tower.

"Both flaps still on?" grinned Obdorsk, his plump cheeks dimpling. "Or did you leave 'em up there?"

"I wish to hell I had," snapped Judson. He felt a sudden resentment against Obdorsk, standing there so fat and comfortable and making light of a subject that was a sore spot with the pilots.

"Sorry," Obdorsk kept on smiling. "I didn't mean to get under your hide."

"You guys in engineering are always getting the ideas," said Judson bluntly. "How long's it going to be before you figure some other way to test those flaps?"

"I understand one of the fellows in Department 6 has got a new design," said Obdorsk. "He thinks he may be able to get oscillograph readings off it."

"Is it just another theory or has he really got it under way?"

"No, he's really got it," said Obdorsk. "He's got the paper work practilly done."

Judson shook his head in disgust. "Paper, paper, paper. Some day you guys will choke on paper."

"Could be," said Obdorsk, still smiling. "How did they feel this time? Notice any vibrating?"

"No, they seemed to be okay."

"How many times did you dive them?"

"An even dozen."

"Speed?"

"All the way from .8 to .94 Mach." Judson answered, giving the speed of the plane in Machs, or in relation to the speed of sound. "I didn't notice any changes."

"Good," said Obdorsk. "Maybe they're going to pan out." He turned and started to walk away. "Well, see you tomorrow."

"Wait a second," said Judson.

Obdorsk halted, his eyes quizzical.

"Sorry about the way I bit your head off," said Judson. "Nothing personal in it. Just feeling a little tired, I guess."

7

"Sure, I know." Obdorsk gave a short laugh and started walking again. "See you in the morning, Jud."

Judson nodded and watched the plump engineer break into a lumbering trot as a yellow plant bus pulled up near the security gate and starting loading passengers. He watched Obdorsk board the bus and then he went into the flight room, opened one of the wall cabinet doors and put his parachute, helmet and leather gloves on the shelf.

Getting his cigarettes from his shirt pocket, he lit up, noticing that the fingers which held the match were trembling slightly. He became aware again of the mild nausea in his stomach and remembered the way he had overcontrolled when he began his initial approach. He swore under his breath and left the flight room. It would be a hell of a note to come down with the flu just when Bixler was getting around to making his decision on who would do those first tests on the YF-188.

As he crossèd the concrete floor of the hangar, passing around the severed fuselage of a Lancer and under the wing of the Superlancer, he thought again about the things Chally hal talked about on the phone that morning. All that chatter about having her hair done and meeting a new ballet teacher with radical theories on leg exercises. But never a word about the important things that he wanted to pin her down on. One question about where she was staying and she was like a trout, slipping off the hook and swimming blithely to some other subject.

He went up a flight of metal stairs and along a hallway to a door on which the words *Engineering Test Pilots Only* were printed in large black letters. He pushed through the door, and let it slam behind him. The lounge was deserted except for Spallanzani, who was lying on his side on the leather divan, arms folded, eyes closed and mouth hanging blissfully open. As he went by, Judson slapped Spallanzani playfully on the fanny.

Spallanzani shifted his position slightly. "Not now, Angela," he sighed. "Not now."

Grinning, Judson went into the locker room where he peeled off his G-suit, shirt, and underclothes. He took a long shower, letting the hard, hot needle spray wash away some of his fatigue and finishing up with a few seconds of cold spray that made his skin tingle. Feeling better, he dressed slowly, tying a careful Windsor in his pleated, russet tie. He rolled up his slacks and applied Kiwi wax to his black flight boots, using the spit and polish technique he'd picked up in Air Force basic, and then rolled the cuffs back down so that to all outward appearances his flight boots looked like ordinary oxfords.

As he slipped into his blue tweed sports jacket, he went back into the lounge and shook Spallanzani's shoulder.

"Hey," he said, "did Bixler say he'd be back?"

Spallanzani opened one eye and grunted. "God damn, what'd you have to do that for? I just about had her stripped down to her essentials."

He closed his eye and rolled over.

"You'll never get her off the ground," said Judson. "Where's Bixler?"

"Ground, hell," said Spallanzani. "It was nice soft grass."

"Did he say he was coming back?"

"Coming back? Who?"

"Bixler, you jerk," said Judson.

"How should I know? He shoved off around four-thirty."

"Thanks," said Judson. He lit a cigarette and opened the door. "Be seeing you."

Spallanzani's hand fell limply to the floor. "Come back, Angela," he called in a high falsetto. "Come back. . . ."

Judson walked down the stairs, crossed the hangar floor and went outside. When he passed through the gate, the uniformed security guard touched his visor and said respectfully: "G'night, Mr. Judson."

"Good night," said Judson.

He strode over to his Jaguar, noticing a nick in the new gray enamel, and as he opened the door he heard a feminine shout.

"Hey, Jud! Wait for me!"

Turning around, he saw Marjorie coming through the gate and waving. He watched her stride swiftly across the asphalt roadway, her suede coat swirling around her long legs, her yellow hair gleaming as she passed through the reddish rays of the setting sun which slanted past the high corner of the hangar.

"Aren't you pretty far from No. 1?" he asked, when she drew nearer.

"I had some reports to deliver to experimental," she said. "Mind if I tag along?"

"How do you know where I'm going?" he grinned.

Pushing the sleeve back from her slim left wrist, she glanced at her watch. "And where else would you be going at five-twenty?"

"Okay," he laughed. "You win."

"I always invite myself when I'm not asked," she said gravely, but her dark blue eyes were sparkling. "Are you sure you don't mind?"

"A blonde like you?" said Judson. "With a figure like yours? Hell, I haven't got a hole in my head yet."

He climbed into the Jaguar, stooping low so he wouldn't bump his head on the convertible top, and put the key in the ignition as Marjorie went around to the other side. When she got in, somewhat awkwardly because of the low seat, he couldn't help notice the way her coat and dress slid up. He caught a glimpse of the top of one nylon and part of a white garter before she swept her coat back down. She had nice legs, not as perfect as Chally's, but nice.

They rode in silence past the outside security gate and along Imperial Boulevard.

"You look a little tired," she said, when he paused for a red light. "Have a hard day?"

He shook his head. "Routine."

"Go very far?" she asked.

"I made Santa Barbara on one run," he said. "How were things at the office?"

"Nothing special." Her elbow brushed his as she clasped her hands behind her neck and leaned back against the red leather upholstery. "This feels good. My, I could ride like this all the way to Tiajuana."

"Sorry, lady," he said, "this bus stops here." He drove onto the parking lot at Ditman's and parked beside Bixler's yellow Jaguar. Then he turned and looked at her. "Besides, you better be careful what you say. I might take you up on that Tiajuana suggestion."

"Is that bad?" Her blue eyes studied him so strangely he couldn't tell whether she was joking or serious.

"With me it would be," he laughed.

She laughed, too, but she joined in a little late and he

thought there was just a slight brittleness to her tone. They got out and walked past the drive-in restaurant to the separate, lime-green stucco building at the rear that was Ditman's cocktail lounge. When they got inside, he could see, despite the dimness, that most of the gang had preceded him. They were all crowded at the bar, except for Bixler who was sitting in one of the leather booths with the redhead he'd been squiring around for the last three days.

Judson led Marjorie to a booth on the other side of the room. As they sat down, one of the cocktail waitresses, the little brunette whose name he could never remember, came over to take their order.

"Hello, Juddy," she said. "The usual?"

He nodded. "But make it stronger than usual and bring the young lady a Stinger." He turned to Marjorie. "Right?"

"Right," she said.

"Care for anything to eat tonight, Juddy?" asked the waitress "The New York cuts are pretty good."

"Sure, bring us a couple, but there's no hurry."

The waitress wrote on her pad, smiled and departed. Marjorie's eyes followed the girl over to the bar and then she looked back at Judson.

"What did she call you?" she teased, raising her eyebrows. "Juddy? Gracious, such formality."

Judson shrugged. "It's her idea, not mine."

"You poor men," said Marjorie. "Chased all the time by females. What a hard life."

Judson shrugged again and she took the hint, changing the subject. "Have you heard from Chally?"

"She called this morning."

"Did she tell you where she was?"

He shook his head. "The same old line of patter. She's having fun, she's got a new teacher and her arabesques and pirouettes are coming along just dandy. I'd like to break her goddamned little neck."

"You know that's a lie," said Marjorie softly. "It's probably—"

She broke off as the waitress arrived with a tray and placed two white paper doilies on the polished wood of the table top. Setting down the two glasses, the girl smiled at Judson and

11

then performed a brief curtsy as he handed her two dollars and told her to keep the change.

"It's probably none of my business," said Marjorie, as the waitress left, "but I think you could go at it differently. Instead of brow-beating her and getting tough with her, you ought to try encouraging her and give her the idea you thoroughly approve what she's doing."

"I tried that," said Judson. He took a long sip of the bourbon and water.

"I don't think you tried it long enough."

"She only got worse." He drained half of his drink and then swirled the ice around in the glass with a circular motion of his wrist, wishing Marjorie would talk about something else.

Marjorie sipped at her Stinger, placed her glass back on the table and began tracing watery designs on the polished surface.

For a long minute, they were silent. Preoccupied with her glass, she did not look up at him again until he offered her a cigarette. She took one and placed it slowly between her red lips.

"I wasn't going to tell you this," she said, leaning forward so he could touch the flame to the tip. "In fact, I still don't think I should."

In the orange light of the match, her eyes were troubled and uncertain.

"Tell me what," he said.

"There's a girl in the office that knows Chally pretty well," she said. "They used to be together in personnel before Chally left. This girl got a call from Chally yesterday and I couldn't help overhear her copy something down. Later, I walked over by her desk and there was this address written on her notepad."

Judson felt his hand tighten on his glass. "Chally's address?"

"I think so." Marjorie opened her purse and got out a white slip of paper.

"Good Christ!" Judson slammed the glass down so hard liquor cascaded onto the table. He stood up, grabbing the slip from her fingers and feeling the anger drawing down his face. "You've had this since yesterday? Why in the hell didn't you tell me?"

Marjorie didn't speak. She looked up at him with an expression that was halfway between surprise and shock.

12

He was aware of a break in the conversation of the gang at the bar and that they were looking over at him. Well, let them look. He hoped they were enjoying themselves.

Without glancing back at Marjorie, he started across the room toward the door.

Chapter Two

WHEN HE GOT NEAR THE DOOR, he had to veer to the left to keep from bumping into Bixler who had turned away from the bar, a glass in each hand.

"Hey, what's all the rush?" said Bixler. "I want to talk to you."

"Haven't got time."

He tried to go around Bixler, but a man and a woman came in the door, blocking his way.

"I want to tell you about those flap runs tomorrow," said Bixler.

"To hell with them," said Judson.

He shouldered his way between the man and the woman and went outside, striding over to the Jaguar. The rear tires spun as he shot across the paving, kicking gravel on some of the parked cars. He crossed Pacific Coast Highway, barely making it on the amber light, and sped down Imperial. Switching on the dashboard map lights, he glanced briefly at the words on the slip of paper, memorizing them. The address was 4415 North Woodington, whcih was a Hollywood street. It made sense, since that was exactly the part of town she'd head for.

On the straight stretches, between signals, he got the coupe up to 70, slowing to 50 as he zigzagged from lane to lane in the busier shopping districts. He knew he was driving faster than necessary but an inner compulsion wouldn't permit him to slow down. Under his breath, he cursed Marjorie for hanging on to the address all that time without telling him. It wasn't

13

like her—usually she was a bright girl, one step ahead of the rest.

The 4400 block of Woodington contained a number of tall, pylon-like apartment houses, ultra-modern in architecture. He parked in a red curb zone near 4415 and went through the all-glass front doors into a pink and silver lobby furnished with a deep rug and low, squarish divans and easy chairs. Near the elevator were a clerk's desk and switchboard.

Judson walked over to the desk, and the man who was sitting behind it laid down a copy of *Emerson's Essays* and looked up. He was a small, elderly man with white hair that had been combed and parted so carefully it still retained the evenly spaced separations left by the comb's teeth. He wore a handsome, peach-colored sport jacket and a light green sport shirt, open at the throat.

"I'd like the number of Mrs. Charlotte Judson's apartment," said Judson.

Turning his swivel chair, the old man opened a drawer and skimmed through a card file. Then he went through the cards a second time.

"She's not in here," he said. "You sure you've got the right place?"

Judson took the slip from his coat pocket and read the address again. "This is 4415, isn't it?"

The old man nodded.

It occurred to Judson that she might've used her maiden name. "See if you've got a listing under Charlotte Falke."

Again the old man thumbed through the file. "Here she is," he said lifting out a card. He looked at it carefully, turning it over and studying the reverse side.

"What's her apartment?" said Judson.

The old man put the card back in the file. "Sorry, young fellow. She don't live here any more."

"There must be some mistake," said Judson. "I just got that address—it's new."

The old man sighed. He took the card out of the file and displayed it so Judson could read it.

"See that red line drawn through her name?" the old man said. "That means she moved out. And those numbers behind it mean the day she moved. She moved out today."

"Then she must've left a forwarding address," said Judson.

14

The old man shook his head. "Nope. Otherwise it'd be written right under her name there."

Judson looked at the card for another moment. Then he sat down on the edge of the desk. "God damn her," he said quietly. "I'd like to wring her little neck."

He continued to sit there while the old man replaced the card in the file and closed the drawer. Then the old man picked up his copy of *Emerson's Essays* and started to read. Judson left the desk and started toward the door.

"Wait a minute," said the old man.

Judson turned around.

"Got a cigarette?" said the old man. "I'm stuck here tonight and can't go out and get any."

As he returned to the desk, Judson passed a cigarette machine that stood near the elevator doors. He looked at the machine and then extended his pack to the old man.

"I know what you're thinking," said the old man. He selected a cigarette, inserted it in a long, golden holder and lit up, gripping the holder delicately with his thumb and forefinger. "Actually, I don't smoke much, but I always figure a cigarette's as good a way to keep a conversation going as any. 'Course, if you think I'm just a cheap skate, I'd be glad to—"

He dug into the breast pocket of his sport jacket and produced a pack. "I'd be glad to pay you back. Here, have one of mine."

Judson hesitated. Enough time had been wasted already and he didn't feel like wasting any more.

"Go on," grinned the old man. "Live dangerously."

Despite himself, Judson smiled, took one of the cigarettes and lit up.

"Fine," said the old man. "Now that we've got the conversation going, I think I remember that Charlotte what-ever-her-last-name-is. She's a little bit of a thing, isn't she, pretty as a picture with those big dark eyes?"

Judson nodded. "That's her."

"She wasn't here very long," said the old man. "Girl friend of yours?"

"My wife," said Judson.

Pinching his lips around the long golden holder, the old man digested this last bit of information carefully.

"Son," he said, after a moment, "if I were your age I prob-

15

ably wouldn't take advice from a potty old coot like me, but even so I'm going to hand you some. But I'm going to keep it short."

Judson stubbed his cigarette out in a yellow plastic ash tray on the desk and tried to think of some way to leave without hurting the old fellow's feelings.

"I've had four wives," said the old man. "Divorced two and outlived two. And there's one thing I learned about women, especially married women. Never chase 'em more than halfways." He shook his white head thoughtfully. "Chase 'em further and they don't have any respect for you."

"I'll remember that," said Judson. He started to turn away.

"Wait a minute, son," said the old man. "You've got a straight way of standing and a look in your eye—sort of an honest, go-to-hell look—that you don't see in young people much these days. So I'll tell what I'm going to do. Half the tenants that move out forget to leave forwarding addresses. Then in a day or two they remember and they phone and we write it down on the card. So if your Charlotte what's-her-name calls, I'll give you a ring. What's your number?"

"Now you're talking," said Judson. He took the pen and card the old man offered and wrote down his name and two phone numbers. "Daytimes you can get me at the Lansdale Corporation. Nights I'll be at home or if I'm not there you can leave a message."

The old man carefully blotted the card and put it in his billfold. "So you work at Lansdale. Got a pretty good job?"

"It's okay," said Judson. "Well, thanks for everything."

Once more he took a few steps away from the desk. Then he returned, taking out his pack of cigarettes.

"Care for one?" he grinned.

"Don't mind if I do." With a wink, the old man chose a cigarette and parked it behind his ear. Then he waved his long golden holder. "Well, good night."

"Good night," said Judson.

He walked across the lobby, out the glass doors to the sidewalk and over to the Jaguar. After he got in, he slumped over the wheel for a moment, feeling the fatigue again in his shoulders and back. It was just like that hairbrained Chally not to leave a forwarding address. Unless she had done it deliberately in case he stumbled onto the North Woodington address.

Angrily, he turned the ignition key. Damn her. It was impossible to figure what she was up to. He drove down Woodington to Sunset Boulevard and parked near the first neon cocktail sign that he saw. It was a typical Hollywood bar with a glass brick and stucco front, and scrubby, driedout cedars dying in a planter box beneath louvered windows. The bartender, a young man with sallow skin, wore a clean white starched jacket which failed to conceal the dirty stains on his shirt. Judson downed one bourbon and water and ordered another.

As he drank, he studied the labels on the bottles in a display behind the bar but his mind was far away. He knew he should be thinking about the flap runs which he would have to do at a lower altitude tomorrow, but he couldn't keep from thinking about Chally. It didn't seem possible that it had only been three months since they had held hands and stood before that justice of the peace in Yuma. It seemed more like three years. She had looked so young and pretty, and there was so much excitement in her huge dark eyes that the JP had refused to believe she was a day over seventeen. It had taken a lot of talk to convince him she was nearly twenty-one.

"Another one?" asked the bartender.

Judson nodded.

After he finished the third drink, he paid the bartender and walked back to the Jaguar. He drove fast along Sunset, cutting skillfully in and out of traffic, keeping his touch on the wheel light and effortless. A traffic light flicked to amber and he accelerated to beat the red and that's when he saw the Chevrolet shoot out into the intersection.

One moment the intersection was clear. In the next instant, there was the Chevrolet's chromium hood ornament not more than six feet away. Judson responded automatically, spinning the wheel to the right and hitting the brake pedal. It seemed to take the brakes a long second to start doing their job. The Jaguar began to turn away but the Chevrolet—its driver rooted to the wheel—continued on a straight collision course without even attempting to veer.

The impact knocked the Jaguar into a sliding turn and it did not halt until it had made a swift, rocking circle and was aimed back in exactly the direction it had come. Judson stepped out and saw that the Chevrolet had gone off on a forty-five degree tangent, winding up with its front wheels against the opposite curb. He walked around to the front of the Jaguar and swore when he saw that the left fender was crushed against the wheel and the grill was twisted and shattered.

Folding his arms across his chest, he sat down on the fender.

In a moment, the Chevrolet's driver, a small, hatless man in a business suit, came bustling across the intersection.

"You ran that light!" he said, running his hands through his coat pockets. "As sure as I'm standing here, I saw you run right through that red light." He turned to the curb where a small throng of bystanders was beginning to form. "Didn't he run that light? Did any of you see him run that light?"

No one replied and the little man turned back to Judson, continuing to run his fingers nervously through his pockets.

"What are you looking for?" said Judson.

"A pencil," said the man. "I've got to get your name and address. That's what the law says—and your license number, too. You had no right to go through there like that. Why—" He swallowed dryly and ran his finger around his collar. "Why, we both could've been killed!"

"I doubt it," said Judson. He drew his pen from inside his coat and handed it to the little man. "We wouldn't even have collided if you had tried to turn out of the way instead of just sitting there."

"Why, I—" The little man's face grew more pale. "Why that's not so! I turned as soon as I saw you!"

Judson shrugged.

He gave the little man his name and address and answered the questions of two dark-uniformed policemen who arrived a few minutes later in a patrol car. Then he went into a drug store and phoned a wrecking garage. After the repair arrangements were made and the Jaguar went rolling away at an awkward angle behind the tow truck, he hailed a Yellow cab and went home.

When he closed the front door behind him, his father stuck his head out of the library door and waved a greeting with his cigar.

"You have supper?" he asked.

18

"Had a steak," lied Judson. He didn't feel like explaining that he wasn't hungry. "Dunc still up?"

"I think so," said his father. "Nice to see you home before midnight for a change."

"A little sleep never hurt anyone," grinned Judson.

"The little bit you get does, though." His father shook his head and started back to his papers as the phone rang.

"I'll get it," sang out Opal, and Judson could hear her heavy footsteps in the kitchen.

"Well, I'll see you in the morning," said his father.

"Right," said Judson. "Good night."

Sliding out of his sport jacket, he draped it over his shoulder as Opal came through the dining room and stuck her grey head around the hall corner.

"Thought I heard you come in," she said. "Somebody on the phone wants to talk to you."

"Okay," said Judson. "I'll take it out here."

He walked back down the hall to the extension phone stand, lifted the receiver and said hello.

"Hello," replied a feminine voice and for a second, for the briefest part of the first syllable, he thought it was Chally.

"I was wondering what happened to you," said Marjorie.

"Oh, hello, Marjorie," he said. "Sorry about the way I ran out on you. I was going to phone and apologize but I just got in."

"You don't need to," she said. "I got over expecting apologies from fliers long ago. Did you find her?"

"No. She'd just moved."

"Oh, that's too bad, Jud. I don't suppose she left any forwarding address."

"No."

There was a pause during which neither said anything. Then Marjorie spoke again.

"Did you get something to eat?"

"I didn't feel hungry," he said. "How was the steak at Ditman's?"

"I didn't wait for it. I got one of the boys to take me home."

There was another pause.

"Say, I've got an idea," she said. "It's early yet, not even ten o'clock. Why don't you come over to my place and I'll fix you a nice salad and a T-bone and we can listen to records

19

and relax? It might be fun. I haven't had a man in the apartment since—" Her voice faltered and then she continued almost as brightly as before. "Not since George was killed. But in your case I think I can make an exception."

"Sounds fine Marjorie, but—"

"You can trust me," she laughed, "if that's what's worrying you. I promise not to ply you with strong drink and I can assure you there isn't a negligee in the house."

"Maybe I don't want to trust you."

"Well. . . ." She hesitated. "We'll cross that bridge when we come to it."

"I'll level with you, Marjorie," he said. "I'd like to come over, but I'm beat. I've been out with the guys every night this week and I better get some sleep tonight or else. Do I get a raincheck?"

"Of course," she said, "I understand."

"No hard feelings?"

"I've told you before, Jud. There are never any hard feelings. But I'll keep that steak in the refrigerator for you."

"It's a deal," he said. "See you tomorrow?"

"Maybe," she said. "Good night."

"Good night."

He replaced the receiver and stared down at it thoughtfully for a moment before turning and walking along the hall. Marjorie was an unusual person, one of the few women he'd ever known that didn't carry her loss around like a heavy cross. Though it was less than a year since George had spun in, she was able to talk about him without dramatics, without staring off into space at odd moments during conversations. Nor did she go the other extreme like those who adopted a phony indifference which stuck out all over. She stood ace high with all the guys at the hangar.

He put out the lights in the hall and then went up the winding staircase and along the upstairs corridor to Dunc's room. Hair combed and face washed, Dunc was standing in the doorway in his red and white striped pajamas waiting for him.

"Hiyuh, Jud," he said, looking up accusingly. "Long time no see."

"Sorry about last night," said Judson. "A few things came up."

20

"A few things are always coming up," Dunc said. "I went ahead and glued the nose block on anyway and I think I got it on crooked. You better take a look at it."

His bare feet padded lightly across the polished hardwood as he led Judson over to the work table on which were spread scores of slender balsa sticks and the conical skeleton of a model airplane.

Judson picked up the fuselage and squinted at it. The nose block was slightly off center. "Looks okay to me," he said. "Just needs a little bit more sandpapering and she'll be ready to cover."

"A fine brother you are," said Dunc. "You don't even lie very good. That thing's crookeder than all hell."

"Well, listen to the old expert," smiled Judson. "I was going to phone you today and ask you what Mach number I was supposed to fly those flaps at. And I was going to ask you about those accelerometer, tachometer and tailpipe readings, too. Too bad you weren't home."

"Aw, you're kidding me again." Dunc grinned, the expression in his eyes showing how keenly he enjoyed being talked to as an adult. "Say, I've got something I want you to see."

He opened the lower drawer in his bureau, brought out his large scrapbook and flipped eagerly through the pages. When he got to the page he wanted, he spread the book open, lay down on his stomach on the floor before it and pointed to a clipping pasted in the center of the page.

"I cut that one out today," he said. "From Aviation magazine. It says how you and Bixler are going to fly the YF-188. Boy, that's going to be a fast one, huh?"

"Confidentially, she'll—" Judson lowered his voice, looked around covertly and pretended he was afraid he might be overheard. "Confidentially, she'll do plenty better than Mach 1 in straight-away flight."

"Man, oh, man!" said Dunc. "The speed of sound just going straight with no dive or nothing?"

Judson nodded. He sat down on Dunc's bed and they chatted about Immelmans and the best way to do a Cuban Eight an da Cloverleaf, with Dunc's small hands simulating the maneuvers with natural skill. It was quite remarkable how well Dunc kept up his end of the conversation. For an eleven-year-old, he was extremely well read on the technical end of

21

aeronautics, spending long hours with the aviation dictionary Judson had given him for his birthday and regularly reading the Aero Digest. There was a lot of detail he didn't understand, of cousre, but he had no pretensions, no tendency to fake information he didn't have like many adults. If he didn't know something, he asked about it.

It was the kind of a give-and-take session they both enjoyed and Judson, watching the changing, animated expressions in the youthful blue eyes, admitted that he probably enjoyed it even more than Dunc. It gave him a chance to relax and be himself because with Dunc everything was either black and white or right and wrong. With him there was no confusing gray area of the in-between. He was scrupulously honest, but this honesty had a curious double standard and it was his only compromise. With Judson, he never lied. However, he often lied to their father, but only as it related to Judson. It was the one bad habit that Dunc absolutely refused to break—or talk about.

"When do you figure the YF-188 will be ready to go?" asked Dunc.

"Maybe in a week. Maybe two weeks."

"You figure you'll take her up first? Or will Bixler?"

"It's up to him," said Judson, "but by rights it's my turn."

Dunc scowled. "That god damn old Bixler."

"Look," said Judson, "if you have to swear keep it plain and simple. You don't need to go around insulting God. Just say that damn old Bixler." He yawned and rubbed his cheek. "Anyway, he's not so old. Thirty-three, only two years older than me. You trying to make an old man out of me?"

"You sure don't act old," said Dunc. "But that damn old Bixler does."

"I feel pretty old sometimes." Judson rubbed his eyes and yawned. "Like during a red-out. A couple of seconds of that and I feel like I'm ninety."

"What's red-out?" said Dunc. "I haven't heard you mention that one before."

"It's something the engineers are starting to bring up a little more often," said Judson. "It's the opposite of blackout. Instead of the blood being drained from the brain like when you do positive Gs, there's a reverse pressure with more blood being jammed up against the brain until you see red."

"Negative Gs, huh?" said Dunc. "Jeepers, have you ever had a red-out?"

Judson shook his head. "Not what you'd call a real red-out. I've seen red for a second or so a couple of times when I was flying upside down. It gave me a hell of a headache." He slid off the bed and stood up, yawning again. "Man, I'm tired. I think I'll turn in."

"Not already," said Dunc. "You only just got here."

"I'm beat," said Judson, stretching. "It's past your bedtime, anyway."

"Aw, hell," said Dunc. "I probably won't see you for another week."

"Sure, you will." Judson picked his sport coat off the chair and started for the door.

"Say," said Dunc. "How much will they pay you for taking up the YF-188? I mean, how much of a bonus?"

Judson paused in the doorway. "Around $4000."

"Jeepers," said Dunc. "That means you'll make way over $21,000 this year, don't it?"

"Jeepers," mimicked Judson, grinning. "You're beginning to sound more like Dad all the time."

"I was just asking," said Dunc, following Judson to the doorway.

"Good night," said Judson.

"Good night, Jud," said Dunc.

Judson walked down the hallway to his own room and as he turned the knob Dunc, still standing in the doorway, spoke again.

"Say, Jud, I didn't hear the Jag come up the driveway tonight."

"I—" Judson pushed the door open without looking back. "I came home in a cab because one of the guys borrowed the Jag. See you in the morning."

"Good night," said Dunc.

23

Chapter Three

HANGING UP HIS COAT, Judson took off the rest of his clothes, put on his pajamas and went into the bathroom. He didn't especially like the expression on the face that looked back at him from the mirror as he brushed his teeth. It wasn't the few prematurely gray hairs that were beginning to show in the dark hair at his temples or the hint of circles under his eyes. It was more the expression in his eyes themselves. There had been no real reason to lie to Dunc about the Jaguar, but nevertheless he had felt a necessity to do so. For a moment, after he'd finished with his teeth, he considered going back and telling Dunc exactly what had happened. But he changed his mind, deciding to explain it in the morning.

When he pulled the blankets up to his chest and switched off the bedlamp, he felt tired enough to drop right off. But he didn't. Instead, the pillow began to feel uncomfortable and he couldn't get it adjusted right under his head. Nor could he find a comfortable position for his legs—they felt tense and restless. And before long he was thinking about Chally and wondering where she had moved to. My wife, he thought, my own wife, and I don't even know whether she's sleeping in a house tonight or in a hotel or a motel. I don't know whether she's sleeping in pajamas or a nightgown or even whether she's alone.

He sat up and reached through the darkness for his cigarettes and lighter on the bedstand. As he lit up, a thought that had been nagging at him for the last hour refused to be ignored any longer. He'd been slow getting his foot from the throttle to the brake, far slower than was reasonable. If he'd gotten the brake down just an instant sooner the Chevrolet would have shot harmlessly by. His mind saw the whole thing as clearly as in a photograph and under the blankets his right foot moved suddenly as if from the throttle to the brake. But in his mind the photograph showed his foot poised uncertainly in the air for at least a second, a ridiculously useless second.

24

He took a long drag on the cigarette and then ground it out in the ash tray and pulled the covers back over his shoulders. The pillow felt as hard and uncomfortable as a football. He turned it over and flattened it with a blow of his hand but it still felt uncomfortable. He wondered if the liquor could have had anything to do with his poor showing on the brakes. Four drinks on an empty stomach, one at Ditman's and three at that joint in Hollywood. It was hard to say—he'd known times when eight drinks hadn't affected him one way or another. And there'd been other times when five or six had sent him higher than a F-160K.

He sat up again in the darkness, lit another cigarette and stared long and thoughtfully at the glowing tip. In a way it was kind of funny how the driver of the Chevrolet had sat there, his hands gripping the wheel, his eyes staring straight ahead just before the crash as if he'd hoped that if he ignored the Jaguar it might go away. The picture reminded him of another face he'd seen one day in 1944, the face of that German in the yellow-nosed Messerschmitt 109. That had been a peculiar one, too. They'd both come out of the overcast at the same moment, at 10,000, both going in the same direction and there was no telling who had been the most surprised. They'd flown wing to wing for at least a mile, neither making a move to attack, and then the German had waved and he'd waved back. In the next cloud, they'd parted company, the ME-109 moving away in a Split S, and that had been that.

Crushing the second cigarette out in the ash tray, he rolled back under the blankets and forced himself to lie still, but sleep wouldn't come. Downstairs the grandfather clock, which needed winding, slowly chimed eleven, its tone flat and unmusical. And after a long, long time it chimed once for eleven-thirty and then a long time after that it chimed twelve, each note coming slowly like a bony finger tapping with great deliberation on a plastic canopy.

When the alarm clock rang at seven, he welcomed it as signaling his release from the prison of his bed. He felt very tired as he walked into the bathroom, as if he hadn't slept at all, although he knew that wasn't true. He didn't feel like taking a shower and somehow managed to shave without nicking himself.

Three cups of hot coffee did wonders for the queasy sensation in his stomach, but Opal scowled at him when he turned down her offer of two fried eggs with bacon. He settled for a slice of toast with strawberry jam, ate it quickly and was rising from the table when his father came through the dining room door with the morning paper.

"Off so soon?" said his father.

"I've got an early assignment."

"I thought maybe we could have a little talk," grumbled his father.

"Tonight maybe." Judson paused at the door. "Is it okay if I borrow the Buick? I loaned the Jag to one of the guys."

He felt a tiny thrust of guilt as he compounded his lie of the night before to Dunc.

"Go ahead," said his father. "I'll use the Cad. I think you'll have to put in some gas."

"I'll catch it," said Judson. "See you tonight."

"Goodbye," sighed his father, opening the paper.

When Judson arrived at the hangar, he went immediately into the locker room and put on his heavy G-suit. Then he walked down the stairs and across the floor of the hangar to the dispatch room under the flight tower and opened the cabinet. He got out his helmet and chute and as he left the dispatch room Obdorsk and his assistant came out of the hangar carrying their usual armload of notebooks and reports.

"Beautiful morning, isn't it," said Obdorsk.

"Real California weather," said Judson.

Obdorsk handed him the test card on which were penciled in a neat draftsman's hand the details of the simulated dive bombing tests which engineering wanted made to check the flaps. He saw by the number on the upper right corner that he would be flying the same Lancer as the day before, but at a slightly higher speed and a lower altitude on the final dives. A glance at the asphalt parking apron showed him that the fighter-bomber was in the final stages of the crew's check-off.

"You may get some substantial buffet," said Obdorsk. "Then again it may only be minor."

"I'll let you know," said Judson.

"Fine," said Obdorsk. He nodded at his assistant and they started up the wooden stairs toward the glassed-in observation room at the top of the tower.

Inserting the test card into the metal clamp on his left trouser leg, Judson donned his thin leather gloves and picked up his chute. He slipped his arms through the straps and adjusted it against his back. He saw Bixler come in through the security gate at the other side of the hangar and immediately turned and started walking toward the airplane, hoping Bixler wouldn't bother him, but quite certain that he would.

"Hey, Jud!" called Bixler.

Judson took a few more steps, then turned around and waited, watching Bixler cross the apron with long, confident strides.

"How come you ran out on me last night?" Bixler demanded when he was still several yards away.

"I had places to go," said Judson.

"Where'd you go?" demanded Bixler.

"It's none of your business," said Judson evenly.

Bixler's narrow, dissipated face darkened with anger and the lines beside his thin nose seemed to grow longer and deeper.

"Maybe not," he said. "But those fancy Cuban Eights you did yesterday are my business. I've told you before about messing around like that—who the hell you think you are?"

Judson felt the fingers that held his helmet grow tense and he had a sudden, almost overpowering desire to smash the helmet against Bixler's face. Realizing that was exactly the sort of thing Bixler wanted him to do, he clenched his teeth and let his breath out slowly.

"You know damn well those Cuban Eights don't amount to anything," he said quietly. "Why in the hell do you keep harping about it?"

"You're supposed to go up there and do the job you're told to do and come down!" said Bixler. "The company doesn't want you messing around with half a million dollars worth of airplane and you know it!"

"Show me a written order from Lansdale himself and maybe I'll listen to you," said Judson.

He turned and started walking toward the airplane again, expecting Bixler to follow and continue the dressing down. When he got to the airplane he was relieved to see that Bixler had also turned and was striding back to the hangar.

"Morning, Jud," said Eddie.

"Morning," said Judson.

27

"She's all set," said Eddie.

Judson nodded and gave the airplane a brief exterior walk-around check, noting that she was outfitted with dummy bombs. Because he knew that Eddie was competent and painstaking with details, he checked only the major items, seeing that there were no hydraulic leaks, making certain that the nose gear emergency accumulator air pressure was at 1200 PSI and pulling the plunger so the nose wheel would be sure to come up. Then he checked the wing slats and looked in the tailpipe for cracks or distortion. There were none.

He went up the ladder, climbed into the cockpit—being careful not to accidentally kick the drop-tank salvo button—and sat down. Putting on his helmet, he pushed the visor up and connected his head-set line, mike and the G-suit and oxygen hoses. Eddie came up the ladder and Judson handed him the safety pins from the canopy and seat ejection mechanisms.

As he began the cockpit check-offs, he felt suddenly weary and when he thought about Bixler's juvenile bickering he felt even more weary. His stomach felt uneasy, as it had felt the day before, and he wondered again if he were coming down with something. If it was the flu, though, it ought to be worse than this by now, it ought to be spreading.

He made certain the landing gear handle was down and the speed brake switch was neutral. He switched the lateral and longitudinal trim, oxygen regulator valve and instrument power to normal. Then he signalled for Eddie to plug in the external power cart, at the same time switching on the generator and releasing the rudder lock. One by one he checked off the two dozen other steps that were necessary before he could start the engine.

He made sure Eddie and the other ground crew men were clear of the intake duct and rechecked that the throttle was off. Then he flicked the engine master switch to "on" and held the battery-starter switch momentarily at "starter" and then to "battery." As soon as he had 3 per cent rpm, he moved the throttle outboard to engage the fuel booster pumps. At 6 per cent rpm, he opened the throttle rapidly to idle and then immediately retarded it, his eyes on the tailpipe temperature gauge.

He waited five seconds for ignition and when nothing happened and it was obviously a false start, he swore, closed the throttle and hit the stop-start switch.

While he waited the necessary three minutes for the excess fuel to drain before he could attempt another start, he leaned back against the head-rest and closed his eyes. He felt uneasy. He pushed Chally to a far corner of his mind and thought about the collision with the Chevrolet. Such a god damn stupid thing to do—and then that lie to Dunc on top of it, the first time he hadn't leveled with the kid. There hadn't been any real need to lie. He could've explained it easily—after. all, accidents do happen—or even laughed it off.

"Ready to try her again?" said Eddie as he came back up the ladder.

"Roger," said Judson.

He went patiently through all the steps again and this time there was ignition and the engine began to roar. He adjusted the throttle until he got 600 degrees on the tailpipe temperature gauge and then moved the throttle to idle and checked the oil pressure and the rest of the engine instruments. At 25 per cent rpm, he signalled for Eddie to disconnect the power cart. When that was accomplished, he signalled for the chocks to be pulled and switched on the radio.

As he taxied from the apron through the wide gate in the security fence and out onto the taxi strip, he noticed that Bixler was standing in front of the hangar watching him.

He adjusted the oxygen mask until it felt fairly comfortable, checked that the diluter handle was at normal and called the L.A. tower. When he got to the far end of the field, he waited for a DC-6 to take off and then checked with the tower again. When he got permission to take off, he switched to channel 4 and told Obdorsk in the engineering flight tower that he was ready to go.

Then he closed the canopy, dropped the wing flaps, checked his safety belt and shoulder harness and shoved the engine up to 80 per cent rpm. Despite the soundproofing foam rubber around his ears inside the helmet, the noise from the engine was tremendous. After turning on the emergency fuel pump, he made a final check of the rest of the instruments and switches. He shoved the trottle to 100 per cent and when the noise was at its most deafening pitch he released the brakes.

When the airplane was rolling down the runway, rapidly

29

gaining speed, he felt the old familiar take-off exhilaration in his chest and felt his heart and breathing quicken. After he had rolled nearly 1800 feet and the hangars and the Lancers on the line were a bright blur, he brought the stick back and lifted the nose wheel off. A moment later he pulled her sharply off the ground, the thrust of her leap pressing him against the backrest. The airplane accelerated cleanly and he immediately hoisted the landing gear. When he was around 155 knots, he got the flaps up and allowed the speed to build into a normal climb. The runway dropped behind, growing slimmer, and sunshine flickered on an automobile windshield far below him as he shot across Pacific Coast Highway.

Already the airplane was outdistancing the noise of the engine and when he glanced again at the airspeed indicator it read 310 knots and the cockpit was almost soundless except for the hiss of the slipstream against the canopy. With his thumb, he depressed the microphone button on the throttle.

"This is 998," he said. "I'm at 5000 going out over the ocean."

Immediately, Obdorsk came on. "How's your tailpipe temperature, Jud?"

He looked at the gauge. "Okay. Between 620 and 630."

"Fair enough," said Obdorsk.

Catalina Island, a long, brown shape fringed with white where the ocean lapped at it, dropped behind. A few miles further on a freighter, looking not much larger than a pencil stub, appeared and then it too dropped quickly behind. As he climbed through the clouds into the clearer sunshine above, he kept depressing the mike button and announcing the changes in altitude to provide the tape recorder in the flight tower with a complete record of all data. He adjusted the test card in the clip on his trouser leg so it would be easier to read.

At 7000 feet, ice began to form noticeably on the canopy and he switched on the de-icing mechanism. When he was at 12,000, he called Obdorsk again.

"Ready to start the first one," he said. "I'll run the card in order starting at .95 Mach."

"Go to it," said Obdorsk.

He pushed the stick forward and the Lancer started down. The wind against the canopy changed from a whistling sound to a howl. And as the speed of the dive increased further, the

30

air became a screech against the canopy and he could feel the automatic pressure adjustments of the cockpit push against his ear drums. The altimeter needle moved rapidly from 12,000 to 4500. He watched the machmeter and when it read .95, and he was approaching the speed of sound, he started to pull her out of it.

Immediately, he could feel the G-suit respond, clamping its pressure tight around his thighs and lower abdomen. The buffeting on the flaps became excessive because of the turbulence around the bombs under the wings and there' seemed to be terrific aileron vibration. He pulled out at around five Gs, holding his breath as the enormous grasp of gravity jammed him down against the seat, momentarily preventing him from moving. He let the Lancer go into a climbing turn and felt the G-suit pressures slacken. He let out his breath and depressed the mike button.

"Large amount of buffet on the flaps," he told Obdorsk. "Plus lateral oscillation of the airplane."

"Any more than expected?" asked Obdorsk.

"No." said Judson. "I'll go back up and run the next one."

"Roger," said Obdorsk.

He shoved up the visor on his helmet and wiped the sweat off his forehead with his gloved fingers as the Lancer began a spiral back to the upper level. With a pencil he made a checkmark beside the .95 on the test card, signifying that part of the test was accomplished and then he glanced at the tailpipe temperature gauge, tachometer, fuel and oil pressure gauges. All were normal.

Chapter Four

WHEN HE WAS BACK at 12,000 he radioed Obdorsk that he was starting again and then once more he pushed the stick forward. He dived further and slightly faster this time, reaching .96 Mach, and although the buffeting on the flaps didn't

31

seem any worse, he seemed to feel more lateral oscillation. It was the same during the next three dives, at .97, .98 and .99 Mach, and as the buffeting increased he felt more and more resentment against the engineers. It was such a lousy series of tests, so god damned unscientific. No oscillograph report, no photo panel report. All he was doing was putting as much strain as possible on the flaps and if the wings broke off instead—well, the engineers would shake their heads sadly and stroll back to their draft boards.

Once more he returned to 12,000. He told Obdorsk he was ready to start the final run at 1.0 Mach, or as close to 1.0 Mach as was practical.

"Okay," replied Obdorsk. "Don't over do it."

"Not a chance," said Judson.

Again he checked off the tailpipe temperature, tachometer, fuel and oil pressure gauges. They were still normal. Then he settled himself back in the seat and aimed the nose down, watching the machmeter so he would be ready for any necessary reactions when the airplane passed through the sonic barrier.

The needle moved around the dial to .90, then to .95 and he could feel the forces building up. The needle moved past .98 and in a moment he was hitting the speed of sound at 1.0 and because of the bombs the buffeting of the whole airplane became tremendous, so pronounced that he could feel the vibrations in his teeth. It was necessary to grip the stick hard to keep the airplane at 1.0 until he had dived to 4000 and he noticed that the aileron reaction was growing sluggish. It took considerably more motion to ease the stick back and start leveling out. The G-suit pressures went up so swiftly, pressing against his lower abdomen like a broad fist, that he wondered if he were exceeding six Gs. He knew he wasn't, at least the accelerometer told him he wasn't, and although the gravity force flattened him hard against the seat for a few seconds there was only a slight tendency toward blackout and he shook it off as soon as the pullout was finished.

"Excessive buffeting of the flaps," he told Obdorsk. "Aileron vibration extremely pronounced."

"Can you see any damage to the flaps?" asked Obdorsk.

Twisting around in the cockpit as far as he was able, Judson glanced back at the trailing edge of each wing.

"They look okay," he said. "Guess I'll come home."

"Roger," said Obdorsk. "How're your RPMs?"

Judson looked at the gauge. "Normal."

"Roger," said Obdorsk. "See you when you get here."

He put the airplane into a sweeping half slow roll and headed back toward the coast. When he was nearing Catalina, he noticed a flicker of movement in his rear-view mirror just in time to see another F-160K diving toward his tail.

Automatically, Judson gave her balls to the wall and did another half roll trying to gain as much speed as possible. A glance at the other F-160K showed him it was flying clean, minus drop tanks and bombs, which meant it was considerably more maneuverable and that, of course, was exactly why he was being jumped. He couldn't tell who was flying it, but he recalled that Spallanzani and White were also supposed to do some testing in this area today.

Because of its superior speed, the other Lancer was closing the gap. In a moment it would be on his tail and he would theoretically be a dead duck. He kept diving until the other airplane was almost in firing position and then he did another half roll, turning upside down for a second. This dive enabled him to approach the speed of sound at around .95 Mach, creating considerable buffet but also providing enough forward motion so his next maneuver—a simple wingover—caught the other pilot off guard and he slid off target, ending the game.

"You silly bastard," radioed Spallanzani cheerfully. "What'd you have to do that for?"

Judson depressed his mike button. "Just to make you eat wind."

"Screw you," said Spallanzani.

"Every man to his trade," said Judson. "You better go back to props."

"Balls," laughed Spallanzani, dipping his wings, "See you at lunch."

They parted company, Spallanzani heading further out over the ocean and Judson returning to the coast. As the exhilaration of the test and the mock combat with Spallanzani dwindled away, he found himself thinking about Chally. He tried not to, it only made him feel lousier, but he couldn't keep his mind off her. More and more these days he kept thinking

33

about her whenever he was flying and he wondered if there were some sort of a connection. His two loves, Chally and flying. A psychiatrist would have a field day figuring that one out.

When he was down to 2000 and nearing the airport, he called the L.A. tower and was told he could come in after a red Convair 300 took off. In a moment, the Convair was airborn and the tower gave him permission. He got his speed brakes out, made sure the hydraulic pressures were normal and then when he had slowed to 220 knots dropped his flaps. He dropped his gear around 180 and when he was properly lined up with the runway, he chopped the throttle.

As his main gear touched the asphalt, he wondered if he ought to go over to the administration building and look up that friend of Chally's, the girl Marjorie said Chally had phoned. Maybe if he sweet-talked her a little bit she might come through with Chally's new address. At least it was worth a try and there might—

It was then, when the airplane was rolling at around 130 knots on the two main wheels, that he heard the metallic pinging sound as if something had broken. He turned his head quickly and glanced at the right flap. He saw it hanging there, broken at one end, and in the same instant he thought about the Chevrolet and his feet went forward on the rudder pedals, hitting the brakes.

The nose wheel came down with a hell of a thump and the whole airplane rocked forward at such a steep angle—wheels skidding on the runway—that he thought she was going to flip. Realizing the enormity of what he had done, he released the brakes, hoping the smoke he smelled was merely that produced by tires scraping asphalt. The airplane bucked and shivered, hurling him against his shoulder straps, and it was only by touching the brakes with a delicate pressure that he was able to keep her from rolling off the runway into the dirt piled up by the construction crews.

With the damaged nose wheel oleo strut vibrating shrilly, the airplane rolled a thousand feet before stopping. Judson's eyes swept over the instruments and gauges, saw that they were normal, and then his shoulders began to shake uncontrollably and he felt cold sweat run down his ribs. He let go of the throttle and the stick and with his head bowed grabbed his

34

knees with both hands, trying to hold himself rigid so the shuddering would pass. But it grew worse, spreading to his legs, and his knuckles became white with the pressure of trying to hold himself still. Again and again he felt drops of sweat run down his ribs and again and again his mind—crammed with mixed-up pictures of the Jaguar's brakes and rudder pedals—tried to account for what he had done, tried to explain it.

But there was no explaining it. Only an idiot would slam on the brakes of 18,000 pounds of airplane rolling at 130 knots.

For long moments, interminable moments, he crouched there waiting for it to pass. His oxygen mask became soaked with sweat and he could taste the brine of it and it made him want to retch. When he trusted himself to sit erect again, he was totally exhausted and sick to his stomach.

Very slowly, with a hand that trembled, he reached for the canopy switch and tripped it. He waited for the canopy to slide back on its tracks and then he wrenched off his helmet and mopped his face off with his sleeve. For another long interval, he stared out the windshield wondering how he could have done such a thing.

Then he replaced his hands slowly on the throttle and stick and taxied off the runway, feeling the vibration of the nose wheel strut against his feet on the pedals.

Eddie and the other crewmen waved him into the parking area. He pulled the parking brake handle and remained in the cockpit for a couple of minutes while the engine idled to stabilize its temperatures. Then he pulled the throttle to off and the engine died.

Eddie put the yellow ladder in place, came up and handed him the safety pins for the canopy and seat ejection mechanisms. Judson had to strain to keep his fingers from shaking as he inserted the pins in the holes.

As he went down the ladder, he realized that Eddie had not spoken and he knew that meant Eddie had seen what had happened out on the runway and was wisely keeping his mouth shut.

He signed the flight maintenance sheet, making a notation about the damaged oleo strut in writing which looked foreign and cramped, and then he started walking slowly toward the

35

hangar. He still couldn't believe it had happened. It was the first time he'd ever had a case on the clanks like that. Even that time over Hamburg when the Messerschmitt shot out all his instruments and the canopy had jammed, even then he hadn't hit the panic button. He'd calmly watched the flames curling back toward the fuel tanks, rammed his shoulder against the canopy until it broke away and then jumped with no more concern than stepping off a curb. If he'd panicked in a hairy one like that, there would have been a good excuse. But there was no excuse for the ridiculous thing that had happened on the runway this morning. No excuse at all. There had been nothing dangerous about the damaged flap.

He stowed his chute and helmet in the dispatch room and lit a cigarette with fingers that still refused to behave.

"Bixler sent word he wants to see you," said one of the men at the dispatch table. "I think he meant right away."

Judson nodded and went out. He halted uncertainly on the step, started into the hangar before he remembered he was holding the cigarette, turned around and walked back outside. He threw the cigarette on the pavement and crushed it with his heel and it was then that he saw her.

Chapter Five

FOR A MOMENT, just part of a moment, he didn't recognize her because she'd had her dark hair cut short.

Then as she came in through the security gate, walking in that easy graceful way of hers, he knew it really was Chally. She sauntered across the apron, hands in the pockets of the tight yellow toreador trousers that fitted her slim hips as smoothly as a sunburn. Two of the guards stood in the gateway watching her with obvious pleasure and one of the crew chiefs, working under the wing of a Lancer, emitted a long low whistle.

She waved when she saw Judson and turned toward him.

He wanted to wave back but restrained himself. When she drew closer and he noticed she was wearing the white sweater that was his favorite, the monogrammed one that outlined her breasts with just a hint of boldness, he felt his pulse quicken.

She halted a few steps away and tilted her head slightly to one side as she looked at him in that way of hers that made her look seventeen.

"Good morning, Jud," she said easily, as easily as if it had only been a day since they'd seen one another instead of six weeks.

"Hello," he said.

"You look like you'd just seen a ghost," she said. "Aren't you feeling well?"

"Feeling fine," he said.

He stepped toward her and she came to him, reaching her hands up around his neck and he closed his arms around her, feeling how small she was and feeling the warmth and softness of her through the sweater. For a moment he held her tightly without moving and then he turned her, his hands on her shoulders, and he kissed her. Warm, almost hot, her mouth responded with eagerness, but too quickly she broke away, wriggling from his grasp.

"Why, Jud!" she said and her huge brown eyes glistened with merriment. "Everybody's watching!"

"Let them," he said.

He caught her hand and would have drawn her close again, but she resisted and he knew better than to try and get her to do something she didn't want to do. So he settled for just standing there holding her hand and looking at her. He liked the gigantic gold loops that hung from her perfect ears and he decided he also liked the shorter hair, especially the way it curled loosely and carelessly at the nape of her slim neck.

"You do look awfully pale," she said. "Is something wrong?"

He turned aside her question as if he hadn't heard it and at the same time tried to ignore the ugly pilot and airplane and brake pedal feelings within him that were still clamoring for an answer to what had happened out on the runway.

"How did you get through the gates?" he said.

"Easy." She laughed and opened her palm showing him a blue company badge. "I didn't turn it in when I quit."

37

"But what about the inside gate?" He didn't know why he kept talking about the gates when there were so many other things he wanted to ask her about.

"I didn't show them anything," she said. "I just told them I was Mrs. Judson and breezed right through."

"I see," he said. "And you *are* Mrs. Judson, are you?"

She looked at him gravely as if she wasn't quite sure she knew what he meant.

"You know what I mean," he said. "Six weeks."

"Silly." She held up her left hand, spreading the long fingers with their scarlet nails, and displayed the slim gold band on her ring finger. "Of course, I'm Mrs. Judson. And don't be so grumpy, Jud. I didn't come out here to have you make faces at me."

"Why did you come then?" he asked.

She looked at him quite directly and then turned, pouting and placing her hands in the pockets of the yellow toreador trousers, and glanced into the hangar. Then she glanced back at him, still not saying anything.

"Why did you come?" he repeated.

"You know why I came," she said. "Anyway, what difference does it make? Aren't you glad to see me?"

"Of course, I am." He tried to keep the irritation from his voice. "But after all it has been six weeks since I saw you. I don't know what you've been doing, where you've been going. I don't even know where you live."

"But I phoned you," she said.

"A couple of times a week," he said. "A lot of good that was."

"But I've been very busy. My new teacher is just marvelous and she says I'm making wonderful progress. Here, let me show you."

Spreading her arms, she went up on the toes of one small foot and piroutted slowly and gracefully, completing two full spins and ending up with a brief bow.

"Did you notice how I held my knee a little higher?" she asked reflectively. "That's one of the things Madame Brouquet has shown me. And did I tell you about the choreographer for MGM studios?"

He shook his head.

"He saw me at Madame Brouquet's. All I was doing was

38

working at the bar doing my exercises, but he said he would like me to audition next week. Isn't it thrilling?"

"Yes, of course," said Judson. He noticed Bixler start down the stairs at the rear of the hangar.

"So I'll have to practice awfully hard to get ready," Chally's eyes began to glow again with excitement. "But just think! If he likes me, I'll be in the movies and you and I can go to one of the theaters where I'll be playing and watch me up there on the screen. Won't that be something?"

"Yes, of course." He took her arm and started to walk toward the gate, hoping to avoid Bixler. But Bixler wasn't to be avoided, leaving the hangar and intercepting them just before they arrived at the gate.

"Morning, Mrs. Judson," he said.

"Hello," said Chally.

Bixler looked at Judson, his face grim. "I want to see you right away, Jud. Business."

"I'll be there," said Judson, continuing to walk toward the gate. "I've got to talk to Chally first."

"I mean now," said Bixler, his tone getting ugly.

"Stabilize your temperatures," said Judson. "I'll be there in a few minutes."

Keeping his hand on Chally's arm, he passed through the gate while Bixler remained on the other side, cursing in a low but clearly audible voice.

"I can't stay very long," said Chally as he led her over to the Buick. "I've got to be at Madame Brouquet's by nine-thirty."

"Sure," he said, "get in."

"Where are we going?"

"No place," he said. "I've got to talk to you."

Chally went around to the other door and got in while he sat behind the steering wheel. He offered her a cigarette and as they lit up, the thought of what had happened on the runway came back again, slicing like a blade into his conscience, cutting him all to hell and making him feel sick inside.

"You're not going to lecture me, are you?" she asked, holding her cigarette in that little girl way of hers between her thumb and forefingers.

"No," he said. He shifted uncomfortably on the cushion. "But things can't go on this way, Chally. You're my wife and

I'm your husband and we're supposed to live together like normal people. How long are you going to keep acting like a child?"

"I'm not a child," she said.

"Then don't act like one," he said. "There's no reason for you to live by yourself. Do I beat you? Do I swear at you? Do I come home drunk and tear up the furniture?"

She looked down at the toes of her black suede slippers and then glanced out the windshield. She did not reply.

"Well do I?" he said.

"You know what you do," she said, still not looking at him.

It was the same old barrier again. He drew cigarette smoke into his lungs and expelled it slowly, trying to think of the best way to go around it. But he knew that there was no way around it.

"I'll make you a promise," he said. "We'll get an apartment with two bedrooms and I promise I won't set foot inside yours until you let me. You can have a special lock on the door with your own key."

She shook her head and the large gold loops on her ears gleamed in the sunlight.

"Well why not?" he demanded.

"It won't work." Her voice was so low it was almost a whisper.

"Why don't it?"

"Because...." She covered her face suddenly with her hands. "Because you'll still try."

"But I promise I won't."

"You promised before and you broke your promise."

"Oh, for Christ's sake!" He flung the cigarette butt out the window and then ran his fingers through his hair. "Why do you have to be so unreasonable?"

"I'm s-sorry," she said.

She turned away from him, still keeping her hands over her face, and he could tell by the trembling of her shoulders that she was crying.

He reached over and touched her gently on the shoulders. She did not try to draw further away so he moved closer and put his arm around her.

"I didn't mean to get you all worked up, Chally," he said quietly.

40

"It's all right." With her fingers, she brushed the traces of moisture from around her eyes. "I'm such a fool."

For a brief interval, they remained together, Judson keeping his arm on her shoulder while she sat stiffly with her hands in her lap. Then she stirred and looked at her wrist watch.

"Goodness," she said, "it's nearly nine and I'll be late for Madame Brouquet's. Will you give me the money now please, Jud?"

"Why should I?" he said.

"Please, Jud, don't be difficult."

"I'm not being difficult," he said.

"I'll need seven hundred this time," she said. "Three hundred for Madame Brouquet."

He lit another cigarette, not offering her one this time, taking time to think as he fumbled with unsteady fingers with the lighter and the pack. He wondered what would happen if he didn't give her the money—and then discarded that idea almost as soon as it occurred to him because he knew that for a girl as pretty as Chally there were lots of ways of acquiring money. Not that she'd ever given him reason to suspect she was interested in other men. But it didn't pay to take chances. And these monthly money sessions at least gave him a chance to see her.

He unzipped the side pocket of his G-suit and reached inside for his leather billfold, his contact with the hoses and bladder of the suit reminding him that he still hadn't thought out what he was going to tell Bixler. Opening the billfold, he counted the fifties and twenties into a small pile in his lap.

"I've got about four hundred here," he said. "I'll have to give you a check for the other three hundred. Shall I make it out to your Madame Brouquet?"

Chally shook her head quickly. "No, just make it out to me."

"It's just as easy to make it out to her," he said, getting out his pen and the single Bank of America check that he always carried for minor financial emergencies.

"No need to," she said.

"Is it because maybe her name isn't Madame Brouquet?" he said. "And you've been giving her a phony name to keep me from tracking you down through her and getting your address?"

41

"Maybe." She smiled, showing her perfect white teeth.

"I guess you know I could wring your neck," he said.

"I hope you won't."

"You know I won't," he said.

He filled in the check and handed it to her with the cash. She placed the check on top of the bills, folded them together and pushed the small bundle into her pocket. Then she glanced again at her watch and started to open the door.

"My," she said, "I'm going to be late."

He reached over and caught her other hand. "Wait, Chally."

"But I'm practically late already." She tried to pull her hand from his but he tightened his grip.

"I've got an idea," he said. "I've only got one more flight today and I can get Spallanzani to take it for me. What do you say you and I make a day of it—take a drive up to Arrowhead, have dinner at the lodge and then come back in time to go to Ciro's for some dancing and drinks. How does that sound?"

She shook her head.

"Come on," he said, "give a fellow a break."

"No." With her other hand, she tried to pry apart his fingers and free herself. "You know what you'll try to do at the lodge."

"We don't have to go to the lodge. We could go to the beach. And I promise to keep things strictly platonic."

"No!" she said, her voice rising. "You promised before and then you always break your promise!"

"God damn it," he said, "I'm no eunuch. I'm your husband, don't you remember? And it's perfectly normal for wives and husbands to do those things, don't you understand? It happens all the time, every day, and people do it because they like to do it, and it's nothing they're ashamed of or——"

"No!" she said, starting to pound his hand with her small fist. "Let me go!"

"I won't," he said. "Not until you give me your address."

"No!" she said. "No! No!"

She got up on her knees on the seat suddenly and with her free hand slapped him across the ear and side of the face, at the same time trying to release her other hand. Then, just as suddenly, she sat down and began to kick at his legs with

42

both her slippers. He held tightly to her hand and tried to catch the one which was flailing around. Once more she slapped him before he caught her wrist. He threw his leg across hers, shutting off the fierce tattoo of slippers against his shins and then she began to scream, a scream so loud and piercing that in the confines of the car it made his eardrums vibrate.

He let go of her and instantly she stopped screaming.

For a split second, she looked at him—her eyes huge and round and strange—and then she sprang out the door and ran across the parking lot to her black convertible.

She started the engine, shifted and drove away swiftly. Not once did she look back.

Very slowly, in a trembling gesture that reminded him how he'd reached for the canopy switch out on the runway, he reached for the inside handle of the door that she'd left ajar. He closed it and as he slid back toward the steering wheel, the clanks hit him again, starting in his shoulders and arms and passing, like the wings of many birds beating against him, down into his belly and then down into his legs. He clutched the steering wheel so tightly he was afraid it would break under his fingers.

And while the shuddering again and again swept the length of his body and he felt the cold sweat breaking out on his forehead, he remembered her scream—the pure, shrill horror of it—and he got so sick to his stomach he had to open the door and vomit onto the asphalt of the parking lot.

Chapter Six

JUDSON REMAINED in the Buick for a long time until the clanks passed. Then he picked one of Chally's large golden earrings up from the seat cushion where it had fallen during her struggle and placed it in the pocket of his G-suit. When he left the car, his legs felt rubbery and cramped, as if he'd

43

been in a sick bed for a long time. He walked slowly across the parking lot, through the security gate and back to the hangar. He didn't want to go up to the pilot's lounge and face Bixler and the other pilots, but he knew he would have to sooner or later and it might as well be sooner.

When he came in, Spallanzani was lying on one of the couches talking to White and Haynes was asleep in the big easy chair. He could tell by the way Spallanzani looked up and then quickly away, that they all knew what had happened out on the runway. He knew exactly how they felt because he'd been in the same uncomfortable position many times before when other pilots had made mistakes. The fact that they were ignoring him meant they knew the error was of considerable size. If it had been a small mistake, they would be kidding him, making jokes about it.

"Well, all night long," Spallanzani was saying, "she kept asking me to put the light on because she had something she wanted to show me."

"So you finally put it on?" asked White.

"Hell, no," said Spallanzani. "I slept all night. I was pooped."

"And in the morning?" said White.

"When I woke up the sun was shining and that was the first time I got a good look at her, being sober and all. She was a typical Manila broad, small and dark, not bad looking. So then she took off her kimono and showed me what she'd been wanting to show me all night. Over each breast she'd had tattooed a word in small, kind of modest letters, Filipino, of course. She said the word over one meant 'sweet' and the word over the other meant 'sour.' She thought it was funny as hell and giggled all over the place."

"Did you test 'em?" laughed White.

"Hell, no," said Spallanzani. "I was already late so I jumped into my pants and got back to the base."

Spallanzani and White chuckled briefly, still not looking at Judson as he walked over to the desk and sat down before the Dictaphone. He turned in the chair and filled a paper cup with water from the Puritas bottle, trying to marshal his thoughts so he could dictate a reasonable report to engineering on the flaps and at the same time trying to think of some way to bring up the subject of his pilot's error so Spallanzani and White wouldn't have to act so damned unconcerned.

"That reminds me of a time I had a row with my wife while I was stationed in Texas," said White. "I went out and got drunk and got picked up by a couple of blondes. One of them had the palest blue eyes I ever saw on a woman, and her friend—the one whose apartment I went to—told me later the other gal had her lips tatooed red because her skin was so pale. I never met either of 'em again so you can't prove it by me."

"She wasn't so dumb," said Spallanzani. "Think of all the dough she saved on lipstick."

"Women are funny that way," said White. "I remember another time in Washington when I ran into one who—"

Judson didn't listen to the rest. Picking up the Dictaphone mike, he addressed his report to the head of engineering and then, speaking in a voice that sounded strained and unconfident in his own ears, he gave a detailed explanation of how the airplane had reacted during the buffeting of the dives.

When he finished, he realized the room was silent and the others had been listening to him. He turned around and saw that Bixler had come in and was standing near the doorway, hands in his pockets, a cynical grin on his thin, drawn face.

"You guys might as well be the first to know," Bixler said. "The YF-188 gets her first test the day after tomorrow."

No one spoke for a moment. Haynes woke up and began stretching.

"Who's the lucky son of a bitch that takes her up?" said Spallanzani.

"They don't know yet," said Bixler. "The bosses haven't made up their minds."

"Any more performance data available?" asked White.

"She's heavy," said Bixler, "around 29,000 pounds, minus drop tanks. But she'll climb straight up—and if she won't do 800 knots in level flight I'll eat my helmet, lining and all."

"Christ," said White, "that's practically 925 miles an hour. You sure about that?"

"That's what they say in engineering," said Bixler sarcastically, "and you guys know they never make any mistakes in engineering."

The room fell silent again and the Dictaphone mike made

45

a distinct click as Judson replaced it in its metal holder. The eyes of the others turned to him in unison, Spallanzani's devil-may-care, Haynes' and White's sympathetic, Bixler's flat and probing.

It was a ready-made moment for Bixler and he took advantage of it, moving over to the desk and setting his jaw in its most formidable first sergeant's position.

"What the hell happened out there this morning, Jud?" he demanded.

"Pilot error," said Judson.

"Yeah, I know that," said Bixler, "but what happened?"

"The flap broke and I hit the brakes," said Judson.

Bixler shook his head. "That's what I can't understand. Why'd you hit the brakes? That flap wasn't any danger and when you hit the brakes at that speed you knocked hell out of the nose wheel, broke the hydraulic lines, even put leaks in the fuel system. That airplane will be out of commission for days—and I want an explanation."

Judson got up from the desk. He looked at Bixler's crooked, sardonic mouth and he knew it would be useless to tell him about all the things on his mind, about how he'd been thinking of the smashup with the Chevrolet and that when the flap broke he'd reacted without thinking. There was really no explanation for what he'd done, just as there was usually no logical reason for pilot errors, something Bixler knew as well as any other flier.

"Well?" demanded Bixler, his tone getting nasty. "What's the explanation?"

"Pilot error," said Judson, stubbornly.

"Is that all you can say?"

Judson didn't reply. He felt the old desire, an almost overpowering desire to ram his fist against Bixler's jaw, not once but again and again. There was no reason for this tirade in the presence of the other pilots. It was done deliberately to embarrass him, to provoke him into the violence that Bixler, standing there making fists at his sides, seemed to want.

"God damn you!" said Bixler.

He seemed on the point of saying something more, but turned suddenly and stormed out the door.

No one said anything for half a minute. The phone rang and Haynes, being the closest, answered it.

. 46 .

"Brother," said Spallanzani, looking at Judson, "he's sure got it in for you."

Judson shrugged.

"He's been out to get you for months," said White. "I think he's trying to queer your chances of taking up the YF-188."

"The bastard," added Spallanzani. "He's jealous, that's all. You can fly circles around him blindfolded and he knows it. You didn't have to stand there and take it like that, Jud. I kept waiting for you to paste him one right in his big mouth."

Judson shoved his hands angrily into the pockets of his G-suit, his fingers touching Chally's earring. "And give him the pleasure of canning me? No thanks. Besides, that was a beaut I pulled out there this morning, a real kidney-busting beaut."

"Accidents happen," said Spallanzani. "Like that redhead I knocked up in Wichita."

"It was a pilot error," said Judson.

"But the accident, the flap failure, came first," said Spallanzani.

"Thanks anyway," said Judson. He put his hand on the knob, opened the door and then looked back at Spallanzani. "How about running that buffet boundary job for me this afternoon? I think I'll go home and hit the sack."

Spallanzani nodded. "I still owe you a couple for those longitudinal accelerateds you did for me last month. Anything I need to know on the boundaries?"

"Routine," said Judson. "Windup turns at 35,000 from .6 Mach to 1.0 Obdorsk's got the card."

"Okay," said Spallanzani. "See you around."

Judson went down the stairs to the hangar floor where Bixler was talking to one of the senior mechanics. He told Bixler he was laying off for the day, received a scowl and a grunted acknowledgement, and then returned to the lounge. Transferring his billfold and Chally's earring from the pockets of his G-suit to his slacks, he changed clothes and left the building. There was still nausea in his stomach and a bad taste in his mouth as he walked across the parking lot to the Buick and when he got in and started the engine his hands felt stiff and unsteady on the wheel.

He had no intention of going home. He drove straight to Ditman's and swore when he saw the sign that the bar would-n't open until eleven a.m., nearly another hour. Getting back into the Buick, he drove down Pacific Coast Highway, watching an F-160K take off trailing thin black smoke and almost running off the road because his attention had wandered from the wheel. He felt restless and uncomfortable. He stopped at a sloppy roadside cafe and had a bottle of beer but it only made his belly feel colder and more nervous and he drove on. When he got to the peeling eucalyptus trees and big red-roofed homes of Palos Verdes, he made a U-turn and retraced his route.

This time when he pareked at Ditman's the bar was open. Except for O'Connell, the grounded Air Force flier who'd been hanging around the last few days, and Hugo, the old bartender with the weather-beaten neck, the place was deserted. Judson sat down several leather stools away from O'Connell and ordered a bourbon and water. He drank it fast and ordered another one.

When the second bourbon and water arrived, O'Connell got off his stool and moved to the one beside Judson.

"Hiyuh," he said.

"Hi," said Judson.

They drank in silence for a couple of minutes.

"Lousy way to make a living," said O'Connell.

Judson remained silent. He tilted his glass up and drained it.

"I said what a lousy way to make a living," repeated O'Connell.

"I heard you," said Judson. He turned and looked at O'Connell closer. O'Connell was younger, about twenty-eight or twenty-nine, with a sunburned face and corroded silver captain's bars on the blue shoulders of his uniform. His overseas cap was on crooked, and his eyes had the soft, slow-to-focus film of a person three-quarters drunk, but he managed to keep his voice almost sober.

"I tell you," said O'Connell, "these jets are no good. They're too damn fast."

Judson signalled to Hugo for another bourbon and water.

"They're dangerous and they're deceptive," said O'Connell. He raised his left arm and bent his forearm in a few inches. "That's all the further I can move it, y' know that?"

"Quit your beefing," said Judson. "You're lucky to be alive after the bonehead play you made, not taking your hand off the throttle when you ejected. You're lucky you didn't tear your whole arm off."

Bonehead play, he thought. A hell of a lot of right I've got to be chewing somebody else out for a bonehead play.

"Maybe you're right," said O'Connell, "but I'll tell you the human body isn't made to stand up under these speeds. These new airplanes, like that YF-188 you pipe-jockeys at Lansdale are going to fly, why, they'll stretch your nerves out like cat gut and then snap 'em right in your face."

Judson shrugged and picked up the fresh drink that Hugo had brought. He wished O'Connell would keep quiet. But O'Connell went on and on, bringing up the Limeys and their jet that required the pilot to lie flat on his belly and then switching topics to the vertical risers that took off standing on their tails.

"You're not listening!" said O'Connell, abruptly placing his hand on Judson's shoulder and bringing his red face, with its odors of stale whiskey, within a few inches of Judson's.

Judson picked up O'Connell's limp hand and placed it back on the polished birch of the bartop.

"I got one more thing to tell you," said O'Connell, "and then I'll shut up. I'm going to give you an example of why these jets are no damn good."

O'Connell raised his hands in front of his face, spacing them about a foot apart. "Let's say these are two jets. . . ." He turned to Judson and squinted. "Now listen to this, Judson, because I got a statistic that'll freeze your god damn heart!"

O'Connell moved his hands a few inches further apart. "Let's say these two airplanes are traveling at Mach 2 and they come out of an overcast on a collision course a mile and a half away from one another. You got that, Judson, a mile and a half away?"

Judson nodded.

"All right," said O'Connell. "At that speed, even with the two pilots looking directly at each other they wouldn't see each other before they hit head on!"

O'Connell brought his hands together with a loud clap and swiveled his head triumphantly around at Judson. "Swell, ain't it, the way the engineers keep moving the speed up? And I want to tell you something else, Judson. It won't—"

"Why don't you shut up!" said Judson.

"I'm getting to you, ain't I?" said O'Connell. "You don't like it, do you?"

Judson picked up his glass and moved to a stool at the far end of the bar, leaving O'Connell laughing drunkenly to himself. Still feeling no effect from the liquor, he drained what was left in his glass and ordered another one from Hugo. As the propeller hands on the mahogany airplane clock over the whiskey display moved to noon, the bar began to fill up with pilots from the Air Force unit at the airport, executive engineers and some people from the public relations department. Spallanzani and White came in, said hello, recognized the signs that he wanted to be alone and went over and sat by O'Connell.

After a while Hugo came back and told Judson he was wanted on the phone.

"Man or woman?" said Judson.

"It's a man," said Hugo.

"Tell him I'm not here."

"But I already said you was here," said Hugo.

"Then tell him I just left."

Hugo spread his wrinkled hands in a gesture of futility, went back to the phone, said a few words and hung up. Judson ordered a steak sandwich and after he'd eaten half of it Hugo returned and said the same man wanted him on the phone again.

"He says it's important," said Hugo.

"Does it sound like Bixler?" asked Judson.

"I don't think so," said Hugo.

Judson swore and went behind the bar through the swinging door at the end, noticing as he walked that his step was unsteady although his head felt clear. The phone was near the cash register. He picked it up.

"Hello," he said.

"Hello, Mr. Judson. This is Charlie Gramercy."

"Who?" said Judson.

"Charlie Gramercy," repeated the elderly voice. "Don't you remember me, the night clerk at the Woodington Apartments?"

"Oh, sure," said Judson, although he didn't remember the name or the voice.

"I called over at Lansdale," said Gramercy, "and they give

me this here number, so I been trying to reach you to tell you that Charlotte Falke you was interested in phoned this morning and give us her forwarding address."

Abruptly, Judson remembered the old man with the well-kept white hair and the friendly way of borrowing cigarettes. He pressed the telephone harder against his ear and placed a hand over his other ear to shut out the hubbub of the voices at the bar.

"You've got the address?" he said.

"Sure," said the old man. "It's 4431 Rolphe Way. That's not very far from here."

Judson tore a blank off one of Hugo's pads of bar checks and wrote the address on the back of it.

"Thanks," he said. "Thanks a hell of a lot."

"Glad to do it, Mr. Judson. And don't forget to drop in and say hello when you're in the neighborhood. I'm gonna talk you into taking me up in one of those there jets of yours."

"I'll drop around," said Judson. "And thanks again."

"Any time," said the old man.

Hanging up the phone, Judson walked around to the front of the bar. He paid Hugo for the drinks and sandwich, folded the slip with the address and tucked it carefully in his shirt pocket. Then he walked outside, relishing the thought of seeing Chally again and wondering how surprised she'd be when he walked in.

Chapter Seven

BUT WHEN HE GOT INTO the Buick he didn't start the engine because it occurred to him that he didn't have the faintest idea what he would say to Chally when he saw her.

He felt a little sick again when he remembered their scene in the car, the way she'd kicked him and struggled as if she hated him. And her eyes—so round and strange—staring at him as if he were some sort of foul animal.

He turned off the ignition key and left the car. With slow steps, he returned to the bar, sitting down on the same stool and ordering another bourbon and water. This time, almost as soon as the liquor hit his stomach, he felt its effect and that of its predecessors. He took the bar check from his pocket, unfolded it and smoothed it out on the damp, polished wood of the bartop. As he stared at the figures and letters, 4431 Rolphe Way, they began to waver and dance and he realized he was potted. With a strong effort, he wrenched his mind off Chally and found himself thinking in unconnected ways about some of the things O'Connell had said. O'Connell was wrong, of course, about the jets being dangerous, too fast and too complicated. Why, hell, as drunk as he was he could remember every detail of the interior take-off check on the F-160K.

Staring at the shot glasses in the rack near the cash register, he began to check the list in his mind. 1—Armament switches off; 2—Landing gear handle down; 3—Engine master, emergency ignition, battery-starter and pilot heater switches off; 4—Speed brake switch neutral; 5—Rudder lock unlocked; 6—Plug in external power; 7—Check rudder, aileron and tail responses; 8—Check circuit breakers; 9—Drop tank pressure shutoff valve off.

He went down the list, checking off each item with a mental pencil, noting exactly where each switch was located in the cockpit. 18—Wing flap lever at hold; 19—Emergency fuel switch off; 20—Emergency jettison handle in. He completed the steps through the 20s and 30s and started in the 40s. 41—Canopy declutch handle in; 42—Test warning lights; 43—Generator switch on. He began checking off the engine starting steps and then he remembered that he'd forgotten something on the interior check.

Again he went through the list of the 40s and he still couldn't remember what it was he'd forgotten and he felt himself starting to sweat in the armpits and on the back of his neck. It was important, damned important, to remember. ... He kept staring at the shot glasses on the rack and they began going around and around, swimming in a blur before his eyes and he realized that he'd only thought they were shot glasses. ... Actually they were clocks and gauges—there was the tachometer up on the right and over on the left was the hydraulic pressure gauge with its red warning area and then there was the accelerometer and the machmeter and the oil pressure and the fuel pressure and the tailpipe temperature and the altimeter and—

He didn't realize he'd upset his glass and was sprawled across the bartop, face in the spilled liquor, until he felt the hands on his shoulders, raising him up. He felt himself being led by Hugo and one of the pilots over to the soft leather booth at the rear. They laid him down and he went to sleep, a pleasant, blurry, relaxed sleep. . . .

When he awoke, his mouth felt dry and there were creases in his cheek from its long contact with the leather cushion. He pushed himself upright, leaning his back against the wall, and looked at his wrist watch. It was nearly three o'clock. His head hurt, with an ache that moved in circles within circles, first at the front of his head, up over the eyes, then in the back near his neck. Quite suddenly he remembered the bar check with Chally's address written on it.

He got up and walked on legs that felt twelve feet long over to the bar. The section where he'd sat had been cleaned up and when he saw that the bar check was gone he had a feeling of panic. He got down on his knees and probed through the rubble of cigarette butts and matches around the legs of the stools.

"Lose something?" asked Hugo.

"That piece of paper with an address on it," said Judson. "D'you see it?"

"I saved it," said Hugo.

He opened the cash register, got out the slip and handed it to Judson. It was curled at the edges and smelled faintly of bourbon.

"Thanks," said Judson. "Thanks a lot."

With the slip safely in his possession once more, his head began to swim and he reeled against the bar for support. He sat down, drank a glass of water and waited patiently for the giddiness to pass. He thought again about Chally and he knew he had to see her and get things straightened out or else go crazy. There was no sense putting it off any longer. He'd handled it badly this morning, hadn't even gotten to say what he'd wanted to say, and it wouldn't do to make that mistake twice.

When he walked out to the Buick, he knew he was only

half sober so he drove with extreme caution, staying under 40 miles an hour, slowing down in plenty of time whenever a light turned amber. The 4431 Rolphe Way address was easy to find—it was only a few blocks from where she'd been living before. It was the same kind of an apartment house, tall and modernistic with a blue and white striped canopy over the entrance.

He had no trouble discovering which apartment was Chally's. Her name was typed neatly on a small strip of cardboard on the directory in the lobby. When he got out of the elevator on the fourth floor and rang her doorbell, he had the same tight feeling in his stomach that he'd had the day he'd put the XF-160 prototype through its first structural integrity test.

The door swung back and Chally was framed in the doorway, light from the windows behind her glinting in her dark hair.

"Oh!" she said and immediately tried to shut the door.

Judson stepped forward, barring the door with his shoulder. "Chally, I've got to talk to you!"

For a few seconds there was pressure on the door as she tried to force it shut. Then she backed away. He slipped inside and closed the door behind him.

"How did you find me?" Her large eyes were bright with anger.

"That would be telling." He tried to keep his voice light. "Let's just say I was lucky."

"You're drunk," she said.

He shook his head. "I was but I'm not now—and I've got to talk to you, Chally. We can't go on this way. It's ridiculous and it's foolish and it's making things worse."

"It can't be helped," she said, walking over to the long, low, watermelon-pink divan.

Curling her legs under her, she sat down, tilting her head at him in that little girl way of hers, her eyes troubled and brooding. He felt a sudden, deep desire to pull her up in his arms. He was sure that if he could touch his cheek to hers, rub it gently, that every thing would be all right between them.

But when he approached the divan, she asked him coolly to sit in the easy chair a few feet away.

He felt instantaneous rebellion.

54

"God damn it!" he said. "Am I so repulsive? Am I such a monster that I can't even sit beside you?"

She merely looked at him, her eyes frigid and withdrawn, and he knew that by exploding at her he'd done exactly what he'd promised himself not to do.

They talked about little, inconsequential things for a few minutes before he was able to guide the conversation back to more important channels.

"Chally," he said, quietly, "why don't we try it again? We could live here, if you like, since it's close to your dancing school and if—"

"No," she said.

"Let's talk about it reasonably, Chally. All it takes is co-operation and a little—"

"It won't work," she said and her manner, the lift in her head was suddenly quite mature. "I can't run the risk of be-coming pregnant, Jud. You know that. It would ruin my figure and Madame Brouquet would be horrified."

"But who says you'll get pregnant? There's no reason to be afraid. Didn't you ever hear of planned parenthood?"

"Please, Jud." She averted her face and began rubbing her long, scarlet-tipped fingers together in her lap. "You promised before we were married that there wouldn't be any children and now—"

"But there won't be," he said. "Not until you're ready, not until you want them. Can't you see it's all wrong the way we're living?"

Continuing to stare down at her hands, she made no reply.

"I know this is a subject you don't like," he said, "but sometimes talking about things is the only way people ever get them settled."

He left the easy chair and sat down on the divan beside her. She did not draw away as he feared she might.

"I love you, Chally," he said quietly. "I love you more than I ever thought it was possible and I'm slowly going to pieces. It's just that you're so young you don't understand all about it. I know now that I was too rough that first night in Yuma, but I'm sure that if we tried it again we'd—"

She turned her head away abruptly and he felt that there was no longer any communication between them. It was as if a plate glass barrier had been thrust between them, a barrier that deflected his words coldly and impersonally. On the other side Chally sat aloof, head held high emphasizing the exquisite line of her throat and he wished desperately for words, the right words, that would let her know how deep his longing was for her.

The words did not come. He got up from the divan, went over to the windows and lit a cigarette. For a few moments, he looked down at the street and then he turned and looked at her again.

Chally leaned against the divan and stifled a yawn with the back of her hand. He watched her arch her back, lazily like a young feline, and fill her lungs with air, accentuating the firm, rising line of her breasts. He watched her touch her hand, with its fingers spread so casually, to her lips and he felt a rush of emotions. He didn't know what it was that compelled him—whether it was the ripe juvenile sex of her or whether it was the utter lack of concern for him that the yawn implied—but he found himself striding back to the divan.

When he dropped down beside her, she turned, startled, and tried to get up but he caught her in his arms. He knew it was the wrong thing to do, absolutely the wrong thing, but he couldn't help himself. He kissed her hard—and was totally unprepared when she kissed him back. It was a strangely wild kiss and the response in it was so astonishing it made him feel dizzy and light-headed as if he'd had a great long gulp of champagne. He touched her right breast with his fingers, lightly stroking the perfect beauty of it, and he could tell that she liked it by the way she trembled.

He kissed her on the side of the neck and he could feel and hear her breathing warm and fast against his ear. When his fingers moved to the white buttons at the back of her sweater, she squirmed against him and he unbuttoned a second and then a third button before he realized she was trying to get away from him.

"No Jud!" she said, her voice tight and small. "No!"

He couldn't believe it. Nor could the thrust of the emotions within him believe it. Like spikes, her fingers drove against his chest, pushing him away. He felt a sudden, giant rage— a culmination of a dozen different ordinary rages that he'd

56

had for weeks—and he brushed her hands away with one sweep of his arm. He felt that no power on earth could stop him from what he was going to do, from what he had to do. With a wrench of his hands, he tore the rest of the buttons off her sweater.

Chally screamed. It was an abortive scream because he swiftly pressed his hand over her mouth. She kicked at him as he fumbled with one hand for the zipper at the side of her yellow toreador trousers and when he had nearly succeeded in opening it she slid her mouth around the palm of his hand and bit his little finger.

Her teeth were strong and sharp and went in to the bone. The pain, sudden and deep, surprised him and he pulled his hand away. In the same instant she rose from the divan with a burst of strength that caught him unawares. She kicked herself free of his other hand, bounded to her feet and ran screaming to the bedroom.

For a moment, he stood there looking down at the blood flowing from the twin deep crescents in his finger. His brain swam in a haze of confusion, frustration and disgust. He didn't look up until he realized she had slammed the bedroom door shut and was standing behind it screaming at the same shrill pitch she had hit that morning in the car.

He strode over and twisted the knob. The door was locked.

"Stop it!" he shouted. "Chally, stop that screaming!"

She stopped. But only for the second required to regain her breath so she could continue.

He knew he had to stop her before she attracted the attention of the neighbors. Drawing back a step, he hurled his weight against the door. Again and again he struck the panel with his shoulder and with each blow Chally's voice seemed to grow louder. The door was strongly built but finally a split appeared in the paneling near the center, the wood began to creak and bits of enamel fell. He drew back for another blow and it was then he heard voices in the hall outside the apartment.

As he turned, a key clicked in the lock of the front door. Before he could cross over and block it, the door opened and two men came in.

The tallest man, wearing a pearl-gray business suit, gestured

57

with a ring of keys and looked at Judson with narrow, suspicious eyes.

"I'm the manager," he said. "What's going on here?"

At the sound of the new voice, Chally stopped screaming.

"Family argument," said Judson.

The manager glanced at the blood on Judson's hand. "Quite an argument, I'd say. Who are you?"

"Her husband," said Judson angrily. "And we can settle this without any outside help."

"I distinctly recall that the young lady registered as Miss Falke," said the manager. He crossed to the bedroom door. "Are you all right in there?"

He had to ask the question a second time before Chally replied.

"I guess. . . . so."

"Would you care to come out?"

She hesitated. Then she unbolted the door, opened it halfway and stood in the doorway, looking first at Judson and then at the other two men with large, frightened eyes. Her white sweater covered her decently enough in front, but her back was exposed where the buttons had been torn off.

The manager's narrow eyes did not miss any of the details.

"I see," he said. "Miss Falke, do you want me to call the police?"

Chally looked as if she did not understand.

"The police," repeated the manager. "Shall I call them?"

Chally shook her head.

"This man—" The manager indicated Judson with a contemptuous wave of his manicured fingers. "This man says he's your husband. Is he?"

"No."

Judson stared at her incredulously.

"You bitch," he said.

"Shall we throw him out?" asked the manager.

Chally nodded.

The manager glanced at his assistant—a broad-shouldered, thick-necked man—and a silent signal passed between them.

The assistant took a step toward Judson.

"Lay a finger on me," warned Judson, "and I'll knock you on your fat behind!"

58

The assistant stopped abruptly and looked to the manager for advice.

Judson crossed the room and went out the front door. When he started down the corridor, he thought he heard Chally call to him, but he did not look back. He went down the stairs, through the lobby and out to the Buick.

The subsequent hours at Ditman's were a long swimming blur of solitary drinking when he fended off all offers of companionship followed by a period when he was the life of the party, lying on the piano and singing, winning bets by cracking ice cubes with his teeth and throwing shot glasses at the photograph of an F-160K which hung behind the bar. He didn't know what time it was when he loaded Spallanzani and a drunken brunette in the Buick and headed down Pacific Coast Highway. The brunette kept yelling for more speed all during the ride to the motel where Spallanzani was staying. When Spallanzani got out, carrying the giggling girl in his arms, he invited Judson into his cabana, explaining with a wink that she wouldn't mind dividing her charms, adding, in fact, that she often preferred it that way. Judson felt an unreasonable desire to accept the invitation, but he fought it down. He turned the Buick around and drove back to the highway.

He returned to Ditman's, had another bourbon and water, and started for home, driving with exaggerated caution, inhaling the stink of twelve hours worth of whiskey that exuded from his pores, smelling the sticky-sweet perfume of the brunette that lingered in the car. He cursed the accusing image of Chally that drifted back and forth on the windshield, an image even the windshield wipers couldn't erase. When he got home, he parked slowly, taking great pains to line the car up with the curb, but when he got out he saw that the wheels were nearly two feet away from the sidewalk. He parked all over again, shut the windshield wipers off, and walked unsteadily up the flagstone path to the front door.

With a minimum of noise, he let himself in and walked through the darkness of the house up the stairs to his room. He threw his coat on the chair, felt his way to the bed and dropped heavily down on it, rubbing his forehead where it

59

ached from the pressures of too much loud talk and laughter, too many cigarettes and not enough sleep.

In less than a minute, there came a light tap on the door.

"Hey, Jud!" whispered Dunc from the hallway. "Can I come in?"

"Yeah," grunted Judson.

The door swung almost silently on its hinges and then there was the sound of small bare feet crossing the floor.

"What d'you want?" said Judson. " 'S late."

"Got something to show you," said Dunc. "Can I put on the light?"

He didn't wait for permission, but snapped the wall switch eagerly and Judson had to put his hand over his eyes to protect them from the glare of the overhead fixture.

"Hey, look!" Dunc shook Judson's arm. "I got the tail on already!"

Uncovering his eyes, Judson scowled at the balsa wood fuselage Dunc was waving in front of his face.

"Pretty good?" said Dunc, proudly. "I sand-papered all the parts, too."

"Chris' sake!" Judson pushed the fuselage away and closed his eyes. "I told you twice not to put the tail on till it was covered. You'll have to take it apart and you'll prob'ly bust it."

"Why can't I put the paper on this way?" said Dunc.

"Tell you in the morning...." Judson rolled over. "Now put the god damn light out."

"You said we weren't supposed to say god damn," said Dunc.

"Go 'way," said Judson. "Go to sleep."

"Gee, Jud, I waited all night for you to come home and I just wanted—"

"Put that light out!"

"Okay, okay."

Dunc walked to the doorway, flicked the wall switch, and went out into the hall. Judson shook off his flight boots and tried to get comfortable.

"Jud?"

This time Dunc's whispered voice came from the hallway. "Hey, Jud?"

Judson tried to feign sleep but it didn't do any good. Dunc kept calling.

"Yeah," said Judson finally.

"The teachers are all going to some meeting tomorrow," said Dunc, "and there isn't going to be any school. You promised I could come out to the plant some day and watch you fly a test and so I was thinking tomorrow we could—"

"No," said Judson.

"But you promised, Jud, and—"

"God damn it, no!" said Judson. "We can't have a snotty-nosed kid runnin' around gettin' in the way.... Guards wouldn't let you in, anyway. Go to your room, damn it.... lemme sleep!"

He heard Dunc walk slowly down the hall and then he turned over and went to sleep.

Chapter Eight

HE SAW IT ALL again with a terrifying, three-dimensional vividness. He turned his head, saw the flap hanging there broken and immediately his feet moved toward the brakes. The airplane was rolling at 100 knots down the runway and the danger was so obvious he was certain the boots would stop before they reached the pedals. For an instant, the boots hesitated and he could see a face—a staring, frightened face, his own face—mirrored in the polished black surface of the leather. With a superhuman effort, he tried to keep the boots from descending, but they leaped away from him with a savage desire to destroy him. They hit the pedals, and he heard himself screaming—

He awoke with a start, a chill sweat running down his ribs, the clanks shaking his legs and shoulders. Rolling to a sitting position on the bed, he grabbed his knees and hung on with all his strength, his fingernails piercing the cloth of his rumpled slacks and cutting into his skin.

It was a long time before the shuddering began to slacken and an even longer time after that before it stopped altogether. Even though he still had on all his clothes, he was cold, ice cold, and after he climbed under the covers he had to clench his teeth to keep them from chattering.

He lay there staring across the room through the gray-blue dawn light that was coming in through the windows and he knew there was no sense trying to kid himself any longer. For two days, he had tried to convince himself he was coming down with the flu when he'd known all along it was his nerves.

His nerves. He reached over to the night stand, got his cigarettes and lit one with a match that dropped from his fingers. He picked it up quickly from the bed-clothes and dropped it in the ashtray. After all these years, it wasn't his eyes or his ears or his heart. It was his nerves.

Though he knew sleep was out of the question, he closed his eyes. It was strange how a man could change. He remembered his senior year at UCLA, taking engineering courses in the daytime and working nights as a busboy until he got the $350 for the operation on his eyes. "Wall-eyes," the Air Force doctor had told him at his first physical. "Double vision." He was glad he earned the money for the operation himself instead of arguing with his father who was against his enlisting in the Air Force. He remembered his eagerness and his pride when he passed the exam the next time. And there were other days of pride—like the morning at Kelley when his instructor had a seizure. Judson had landed the trainer without a bobble, although it was so early in his training he hadn't made practice landings beforehand. His hands hadn't trembled once during the landing—or afterward.

And there were those other times, the long months of sorties over North Africa, Italy and Southern France. Folke-Wolfes and Messerschmitts. Days on end when there was little or no sleep. Sortie after sortie and yet he always had a steady hand, even during the hairiest ones. Fourteen confirmed and eleven probables. And five more kills in Korea, even though he was nearly thirty then. But he'd had a clear eye and un-trembling fingers, even when the three MIGs shot out his hydraulics and chased him down to tree level over Hungnam.

He lit another cigarette, watched the room grow lighter as the sun came up, and tried to think back to when things had

62

first started to go wrong. He wondered if it could really have started the previous month when he'd made those rocket tests with Spallanzani and they'd nearly collided. He shivered, recalling how Spallanzani's wing had touched his stabilizer, leaving a perfectly straight scratch two feet long in the metal surface. He hadn't gotten over that one with the old casualness. In the days that followed, he'd thought about it a lot, though Spallanzani had never mentioned it.

The cigarette tasted bad. He sat up in the bed, still feeling cold, and crushed the butt out in the ashtray. And then he did something he hadn't done for a long time. He held his hands in front of his face and he looked at them, looked at them closely.

They were square hands, strong, with callouses. They were a young man's hands but this morning they were an old man's hands. They were shiny with sweat and each finger, especially the one Chally had bitten, displayed individual tremors. He tightened the tendons until each hand was a claw—and still they trembled.

He turned suddenly and slammed his fist into the pillow. Again and again he struck the pillow, struck it because he was thirty-one years old and soon to be thirty-two, struck it because of the clanks, struck it because O'Connell was right, struck it because the jets were too fast and complicated, struck it because mistakes happened too often. And then he struck it one last hard blow, the hardest of all, because he was afraid—he was so afraid that now he was even willing to admit he didn't like to fly any more.

He didn't get up until he heard the alarm clock's faint ringing in his father's room. He stripped off his wrinkled slacks and his sweat-stinking, whiskey-stinking shirt and took a shower, staying under the spray for a long time until some of the tone returned to his muscles. When he started to shave, his fingers felt steadier but nevertheless he nicked himself beside his mouth.

As he went down the stairs, he heard voices in the dining room, his father's and Dunc's, and they were talking about him. He didn't want to eavesdrop but they gave him no choice.

"I thought it was after twelve," his father was saying.

63

"No," said Dunc, "he got in before, maybe it was eleven-thirty or so."

"Had he been drinking?"

"Uh, uh," said Dunc. "I don't think so."

"I don't like it," his father said, "I don't like the way he's been acting all week. Are you sure he hadn't been—"

His father stopped talking as Judson entered the dining room and buried his nose in the morning paper.

"Morning," said Judson.

"Good morpning," said his father, looking up too quickly, his round pink face doing a poor job of pretending that he hadn't been talking about Judson.

"Hiyuh, Dunc," said Judson.

"H'lo," said Dunc. He kept his eyes averted as he dug into his grapefruit and he did not look at Judson or speak to him during the remainder of the meal.

While he drank his coffee, Judson tried to think of some way to let Dunc know he was grateful for the way he hadn't told their father he'd been drunk the night before. But there was no opportunity. Nor was there an opportunity to explain why he didn't want Dunc at the plant today.

Finishing his toast, he said goodbye and went out to the Buick. He drove to the plant, his stomach growing tense as soon as he saw the line of parked F-160Ks, and walked up to the pilot's lounge. With a small sense of relief, he learned from White that Bixler wouldn't be around because he was spending the day at Edwards Air Force Base. He thumbed through the test cards on the desk and saw that he'd been assigned a gloved leading edge evaluation and a functional with stalls at 15,000. That was the one consolation he got from the damage on the airplane he'd flown yesterday—at least he wouldn't have to do any more flap tests for a while.

The door slammed open and Spallanzani came in, on time for a change, a big grin on his dark Latin face.

"Boy, you should have taken me up on that invite!" He slapped Judson on the shoulder. "That gal did it every way but standing on her head."

"I'm disappointed in you," said White. "I thought you always did it standing on your head."

"Up you," grinned Spallanzani. He turned back to Judson.

"You look pale, puny and peaked, boy—what's the matter, off your feed?"

Judson shrugged. "Got a touch of the flu, I guess."

"I've been meaning to ask you, Jud," said White, "what's happened to your Jag? Haven't you been driving a Buick the last couple of days?"

Judson hesitated only briefly. "It's in the shop. Radiator sprung a leak."

"New car like that?" said White. "That's a hell of a note."

"Yeah," said Judson. "I was pretty disappointed because the—"

He was grateful for the voice of the dispatcher which interrupted on the inter-com.

"Spallanzani in?" asked the dispatcher.

"Like Flynn," said Spallanzani, depressing the inter-com button on the desk.

"No. 978's on the line waiting," said the dispatcher. "If Jud's around, put him on."

Judson leaned over the desk. "This is Jud."

"No. 966 isn't going to be ready today. So they're going to give you one of the Js with the same leading edge, but it won't be ready until ten o'clock. We'll let you know."

"Okay," said Judson.

While Spallanzani and White changed their clothes in the locker room, he lay down on the leather divan and in his mind went over the control and instrument differences on the J. The F-160J was essentially the same airplane as the F-160K, except that it was faster because of the afterburner. Some of the markings on the left and right consoles were different and he made a mental note to remember that there were additional manual releases on the center pedestal.

"The wild blue awaits," said Spallanzani as he and White came out in their G-suits. "See you later."

"So long," said Judson.

After they left, he got up from the divan, went over to the windows and looked down at the Lancers on the line. He watched Spallanzani go up the ladder and into the cockpit of an F-160K and then he turned away from the windows and went back to the divan. He didn't like the delay. He caught himself rubbing his thumb back and forth nervously over his knuckles and made himself stop it.   At five minutes to ten, the dispatcher came back on the inter-com and told him the test would be delayed until one o'clock because the J's emergency fuel system needed rechecking.

He got out the factory manual on the J and read through it until Spallanzani and White came back and they went to lunch together at Ditman's. The other two drank scotch with their steak sandwiches but Judson ordered a beer and drank only half of it.

When they returned to the pilot's lounge, Spallanzani and White left almost immediately for a simulated rocket run. Haynes came in from Edwards, chatted a little while, and departed again. At two-fifteen, the dispatcher said the J was nearly ready, but he called again in five minutes and said there would be more delay because of additional trouble in the emergency fuel system.

Judson's belly felt taut and gaseous. He rubbed his hands on his slacks, drying the sweat off the palms, and tried to keep his mind off yesterday's mishap. But his mind settled on Chally and the expression on her face when she'd told the apartment manager that he wasn't her husband—and that was worse than thinking about the louse-up on the runway. He went to the phone and started to dial engineering, ready to tell them he was sick, ready to give them any excuse to get out of taking up the J, and it was then that the dispatcher came back on the inter-com.

"Jud?" he said. "You still there?"

Judson hung up the phone and went over to the inter-com. "Still here," he said.

"Good. She's finally ready to roll. Shall I tell them you'll be right over?"

"Yeah," said Judson.

When he was in his G-suit, carrying his helmet and chute and walking out to the line, he had a sudden feeling of dread as he looked at the J. Its configuration was the same as the F-160K's, except for the rounded black radar hood over the intake duct and the slightly greater bulge aft for the afterburner. He knew exactly where every control was, the location of every switch and clock, but he didn't like it. He didn't like the way he felt. As he walked along, his flight boots making gritty, sand-crushing noises on the aspalt, he was struck by the incongruity of it all and he wondered why he should be walking toward this sleek, dangerous swept-back object instead of toward the safety of a plain ordinary factory job, or a garage job or a department store job like all the other snug, secure people in the world.

The crew chief came down the ladder from the cockpit, shaking his head and cursing. He looked up as Judson approached.

"What a pain in the butt," he commented scowling into the J's intake duct.

"What was wrong?" said Judson.

"Dirt in a fuel line," said the crew chief. "Couldn't blow it out, couldn't suck it out, had to take the whole god damned thing apart. But it's okay now, clean as a flea's ear."

"Thanks," said Judson. "Where's Eddie today?"

"They sent him up to the desert. They're working like hell to get the YF-188 ready."

Judson nodded. He gave the airplane a complete, exterior walk-around check, inspecting even the condition of the tires and looking for such minor things as loose rivets, items he didn't bother with when Eddie was on the job. Then he put on his helmet and his chute, went up the ladder and got into the cockpit. After he connected his head-set line, mike and the oxygen and G-suit hoses, he went carefully over all the interior check-offs, turning on switches, closing others, trying unsuccessfully to ignore the unsteadiness of his fingers and the zero sensation in his belly.

He handed the safety pins from the canopy and seat ejection mechanisms to the crew chief and then went step by step through the process of starting the engine. Ignition occurred almost immediately and the mixed roar and whine of the turbines pounded in his eardrums despite the soundproofing of the helmet.

Finishing the rest of the instrument check-offs, with all readings normal, he taxied out onto the taxi strip and contacted the tower. He didn't have to wait when he arrived at the take-off point on the runway but got an immediate okay from the tower. He forced himself to sweep all the trash from his mind, the cluttered thoughts about the brake incident the day before, the thoughts about Chally, the fear of the clanks. He turned on the afterburner and revved everything up to 100

67

until the cockpit became a solid mass of vibrations and thunder. Then he released the brakes.

With the added kick from the afterburner, the J gained speed swiftly. He didn't know what it was, maybe it was the stimulation from the oxygen, but he began to feel better as soon as she was airborn. He pointed her nose up sharply, got the gear up, then the flaps, and called Obdorsk in the engineering flight tower.

"This is Jud in 971. I'll check in again when I'm over San Nicolas."

"Okay," said Obdorsk. "How's your tailpipe temp?"

"All right. Around 615."

"Fair enough," said Obdorsk.

Some of the tension left him as the airplane climbed easily through scattered clouds to 15,000 feet. He ran into gusty wind over Catalina, but the air steadied when he approached San Nicolas Island. The sun, which was close to setting, cast zigzag patterns of pale orange light across the surface of the ocean far below.

He depressed the mike button on the throttle and called Obdorsk. "Ready to start. I'll do an accelerated stall first."

"Roger," said Obdorsk.

Flicking on the instrumentation master switch, he checked the test card on his knee and saw that they wanted the data recorded at four frames a second. He adjusted the camera selector switch and then gradually cut the J's speed until he was approaching 180 knots.

He dropped his gear and flaps, felt immediate drag and a light, general buffet on the entire airplane. As he went up into the stall, he kept his eyes on the air speed indicator. He touched the trigger button on the stick and began to record as he decreased his speed as close as possible to one knot per second. The buffeting intensified and the airplane pitched a little as the nose went up. After the stall, the nose dropped straight through without much roll and he was pleased with the way she had responded. And, he admitted to himself, he was also pleased with the way he had handled her because he knew he had cut the speed almost exactly at one knot per second.

As he climbed back to 15,000 again, he called Obdorsk. "Good response. I'll do another stall and then try a few Gs."

"Fine," radioed Obdorsk. "How's the tailpipe?"

Judson's eyes swept the clocks. "Looks pretty good, although a little on the cool side but—"

The white needle on the fuel pressure gauge caught his attention. It was fluctuating erratically and as he watched it dipped down to 100, the lowest mark on the green safety area, and then quivered to 20 PSI in the red danger zone. At the same time, the engine roughened and he could feel a loss of power.

"Fuel pressure gone," he told Obdorsk, trying to keep his voice normal, and then he forgot about the radio and Obdorsk when he saw that the tailpipe temperature was also decreasing rapidly.

He twisted his head around, saw black smoke pouring from cause for panic, and saw that he was pulling only 70 per cent although the throttle setting was at nearly 100.

A dozen thoughts sped through his brain at once—main fuel regulator failure, dirt in the line, too bad Eddie wasn't on ground crew, got to turn on emergency system. . . . He flipped the emergency fuel switch and waited five seconds. His eyes swept the clocks again and he saw that the tailpipe temperature gauge, which had been cold a minute before, was growing hotter. Like a semaphore flag, the needle tilted up to 630 degrees then to 760 and on up into the high red area, pegging at 1000.

Quite suddenly he realized that among the mixture of sounds in the cockpit was Obdorsk's voice on the radio.

"Jud? Come in, Jud!"

Judson tripped the mike button. "Overheating fast. May have to—"

The red fire warning light winked on. Not the aft light but the forward light, the extreme danger light. Immediately, he cut his power but the light continued to glow like a bloodshot eye.

He twisted his head around saw black smoke pouring from the airplane and he knew he'd had it.

His hands were shaking and his nerves felt like they were being drawn tightly from his body. He chopped the trottle to off, hit as many switches on the instrument panel as he had time for, lowered his head as far down in the cockpit as he could, and tripped the lever on the seat handgrip.

He felt the explosion in the seat above and behind him as the canopy was blown off.

Wind whipped into the cockpit, tearing at his oxygen mask and shoulders.

He removed his feet from the rudder pedals, planted them firmly in the seat stirrups, put his head back against the head-rest, and braced himself.

He triggered the handgrip lever again.

It was if he'd been struck in the spine by an immense boot. His teeth smashed together from the force of the blow and his head felt like it was being flattened down on his shoulders.

Then there was a terrific buffeting of wind on his clothes and a shrieking of air around his helmet as the seat carried him upward.

Wind billowed inside one of his gloves and snatched it from his hand.

Lazily, the seat began to make a slow turn and he tasted blood in his mouth and caught a glimpse of the airplane flying a straight course about sixty feet below and ahead of him, the cockpit looking strangely empty.

The seat cartwheeled and above the sound of the air rushing around him he thought he heard an explosion.

He screwed his head around, his hand clawing at the chute and finding the rip cord, and then he saw an access door go sailing by and when he started to turn over again he saw that the J was a greasy black cloud of churning smoke and fire mixed with torn oblongs of metal.

He kept one hand on the rip cord and broke his safety belt and seat shoulder harness connections with the other hand.

Kicking hard on the stirrups, he separated himself from the seat.

He wanted to pull the rip cord and find out if the chute was okay, but he knew he should free-fall at least a thousand feet until his speed had slowed sufficiently so there would be no damage to the chute.

He tried to count but gave up when he reached four because of his concern about the chute.

He waited a few more seconds and that was the extreme limit of his patience. He jerked the cord.

For a long, long second it didn't seem that anything was happening and then there was an enormous wrenching shock on the harness that nearly crushed his ribs down around his lungs.

When he looked up and saw the clean white umbrella swaying overhead, every panel intact, he started to breath again.

Chapter Nine

HE DRIFTED down slowly, unable to see the ocean for a while because of a great bank of purplish cirro-stratus clouds which was moving in below him. The wind blew through the shroud lines, making eerie musical sounds and he was reminded briefly of a Sunday afternoon long before when as a boy he had sneaked up to the altar in the Shortridge Memorial Church and had experimented with the pipe organ, his untrained fingers striking high strange notes.

As soon as he dropped into the clouds he was in a different world, silent and misty white. It was a tremendously thick layer of clouds and he strained his eyes trying to see the shore line or a fishing boat or the tip of San Nicolas Island.

But the clouds were too thick and they followed him all the way down. When he finally broke out of the mist, he found himself only a few hundred feet above the sea and the long rolling swells, dark blue except where they were speckled with reddish-orange from the setting sun, looked ugly and ominous. He kicked his legs, swinging himself in a 360-degree circle in the harness, and tried to catch a glimpse of land, any land, but he saw none, even after he raised the tinted visor of his helmet.

In his stomach there were new overtures of panic because this landing wouldn't be an easy one on dry dirt like his jump in '45 near Hamburg. He ran his fingers over the stiff canvas of the chute's seat section behind him and made certain his survival pack was still attached.

When he was about fifty feet above the water, he felt sweat running down his neck in a steady cold stream. He unfastened

71

his oxygen mask, removed his helmet and dropped it because he didn't want any additional weight dragging him down. Trailing the oxygen hose, the white helmet looked like a small bomb as it plummeted down, hitting the water with a splash that made him shudder.

The water came closer and he could see spray whipped from the crests by the wind. When he was six feet up, he broke the harness and slipped free of the chute. He plunged in over his head and the water was so cold, so god damn shockingly cold when it hit his perspiring skin, that he yelled like a fool and swallowed a mouthful. He bobbed to the surface choking and coughing, found the survival pack and after a fumbling false start got the oneman dinghy inflated. He tried to crawl in over the fat yellow rubber flank but a heavy swell knocked the dinghy away from him.

Swimming sluggishly because of the water-logged weight of his G-suit, he caught up with the dinghy, got a tight grip on it and dragged himself in.

He lay there tasting a mixture of blood and salt water in his mouth, his feet hanging out over the edge of the small dinghy, and he began to shake and shudder. And the more he strained against them, and the harder he gripped the sides of the dinghy, the worse the clanks became.

It was a long time before the really bad shuddering passed. When he tried to sit up, he felt so weak he was afraid he might roll off the dinghy. Sharp points of spray struck his cheeks and eyes when he raised his face and tried to look for land. He was unable to see over the waves. The dinghy rose and fell irregularly and each time he raised up and tried to look around, the dinghy seemed surrounded by higher and higher crests arranged in uneven steps like ranges of mountains.

Not that it would have done any good even if he had been able to see over the waves. The clouds which he had descended through were settling down on the surface as fog, blotting out what was left of the evening sun.

Fingers blue from the cold and wet, he peeled the plastic cover from the small signal radio, realizing he hadn't had a chance to tell Obdorsk he was bailing out.

He swore. The radio was smashed all to hell, its split case

revealing broken tubes and tangled wires. It had probably been struck some way during the ejection. The flashlight was in the same miserable condition, its lens and bulb crushed.

He rolled over on his back and looked up at the fog bank, hoping to see patches of sky. By now, Obdorsk and the others at Lansdale would have alerted Haynes and White who'd been running a test around Oxnard and they should be down here hunting him. He licked his lips, tasting the blood where he'd bitten his tongue when the seat had walloped him, and swore again. Fat chance they'd have of finding him with all these god damn clouds and fog.

The wind went through his wet clothes like an icy blade, freezing him to the marrow. He'd lost one of his flight boots when he'd first tried to scramble into the dinghy and his left foot was numb from the cold. He shivered uncontrollably tried to listen for the sound of a jet engine and swore again and again because the slopping sound of the waves against the dinghy's sides obliterated all other sounds.

As it grew dark, he tried to remember how far off San Nicolas Island he was when the engine began to overheat. It had been about twenty to thirty miles, but he'd continue west while he'd tried to get the engine under control and his speed had carried him at least another ten miles out. Recallin how close it had been, how the plane had exploded only seconds after his ejection, he sucked in his breath and shuddered, seeing the control panel again, feeling his hand on the throttle watching the tailpipe temperature needle peg at 1000. He remembered turning on the emergency fuel system and it was then, as clearly as if he were doing it again, he remembered that he hadn't cut the throttle soon enough.

Jesus Christ in heaven! He groaned the words through his teeth.

He'd switched on the emergency fuel system while still at full throttle. As if it were printed in large letters on his brain, he remembered the sentence in the J manuel: *Do not turn on emergency fuel switch without first retarding the throttle to idle.* No wonder the J had blown up with all that fuel spraying around.

He clapped his wet hand across his eyes, his fingers squeezing his temples as if that very pressure could shut the image of the open throttle from his brain. Over and over again he cursed himself, cursed his mind, cursed his fingers, cursed his nerves, cursed the sick nausea inside. How could he have done such a thing? Blown up $500,000 worth of airplane because he hadn't been thinking straight. Eyes tightly shut, his head a vortex of instruments and switches spinning in blackness and pain, he rocked from side to side in the dinghy, not caring if he dumped himself out.

That feeling passed too, finally, and weak and exhausted he lay on his back staring up through fog at the dark night which was folding in. As the fog thickened, and he realized it would be a long time until he was found, the wind slackened and he was grateful for even this small favor. Gradually the choppy waves became smooth swells and there was no longer any spray hitting him in the face and flooding the interior of the dinghy.

He flailed his arms, slapping his hands against his shoulders and then his legs in an effort to restore the circulation in his numbed limbs. But he stopped the exertion after a while because it only exhausted him and failed to bring warmth. Again and again as the hours dragged by, he found himself staring at the luminous dial of his wrist watch, a ridiculous gesture since the hands always read 4:32, the moment he'd ejected himself. He cursed the manufacturer who'd guaranteed it to be shockproof.

He lost all sense of time. There was no longer any sensation in his feet and he could feel the numbness spreading almost inch by inch up his legs. He found himself gliding in and out of unconsciousness as if it were a dark stocking cap that could be pulled on and off. There were times when he dreamed about Chally, dreamed about the elfin look in her eyes when she was happy, dreamed about the warmness of her in bed that first night in Arizona, the warm whiteness of her thighs, the warm softness of her breasts, the warm fragrance of her breath. Then the dream became a cold nightmare that intruded with images of how she had changed, how she'd shunned him so soon afterward, and he awoke shivering and chattering, cursing the damp chilling fog that soaked into every pore.

But soon he was off in another dream, feeling the warmth of the cockpit, feeling the wonderful hot air of the heater. But there was still another intruder, a nightmare of the open

74

throttle, an enormous open throttle with a grooved black hand-grip that attacked him, clubbing him for his stupidity. And again he awoke, shouting this time at the top of his lungs and rolling back and forth on the dinghy until his hands and feet were soaked where they extended over the sides.

When he got a grip on himself, he lay rolled up in a tight ball. He felt cold. He felt as if his muscles were wasted away and his bones were calcified and stiff with age. He was too old and the jets were too young. Electronics. All electronics. And he hated electronics. Packed in tightly in every square inch of space from nose to tail. Too complicated for an old man. *I'll never fly again,* he said, his lips moving coldly against the wet rubber of the dinghy. *I'm all through. Too old. Too god damned old.*

He pinched himself, trying to keep awake, but it was no use and soon he slipped again into unconsciousness.

He dreamed that they were trying to make him fly. They were stubborn about it. They were carrying him to the airplane and demanding that he get in and he was cursing them and railing at them.

"Take it easy, fella!" somebody said. "You're gonna be okay. Calm down!"

At the sound of the voice, he opened his eyes and saw a big wing overhead, saw it so distinctly he could count the rivets on its under side. It was morning and the sunlight was so brilliant it hurt his eyes.

He was being lifted from the bobbing yellow dinghy into the doorway of a dark blue Coast Guard PBM by two sailors with young sunburned faces. They were holding his arms and with a final heave they boosted him inside and placed him on the floor. One of the sailors dragged the dinghy inside and stowed it aft while the other one slammed the door and the pilot revved up the engines.

75

Chapter Ten

JUDSON TRIED TO SPEAK, tried to thank them, but couldn't get the words out.

"Take it easy," repeated one of the sailors, the one with the white cap tilted down over his coppery eyebrows. "You're gonna be okay."

Quickly they stripped the soaking G-suit, shirt and shorts from his shivering body. They dried him with a soft towel, wrapped him in many clean blankets and placed him in a metal bunk. They brought him steaming coffee in a thick mug and held it for him while he drank because his own hands were too unsteady. As soon as the wonderful fluid was inside and the warmth of the blankets took effect, he went to sleep.

When he awoke a long time later, he found himself in a high, spotless bed in a white room with a nurse bending over him. She was pleasantly fat, quite young and wore glasses.

"Good evening, Mr. Judson," she said. "Did you have a nice rest?"

"Sure—" He coughed up some phlegm. "Sure did."

"Since I know you're going to ask," she said, "I'll tell you you're in the Lansdale Corporation Hospital and—" She glanced at her lapel watch. "And it's exactly seven-fourteen p.m."

Judson grinned. "Thanks."

He started to sit up and the nurse gently pushed him back down again.

"Not so fast, Mr. Judson," she said. "You had a lot of exposure and shock, you know."

"I feel okay," he said, sitting up and moving over to the other side of the bed so she couldn't push him down again. "Bring me a gallon of coffee and a steak and then I'll get out of here."

"You will *not*," she said firmly. "You'll eat two soft boiled

76

eggs and, if you behave, I may talk the doctor into letting you have a cup of tea."

"Tea?" said Judson. "Ugh! How about making that a double bourbon and water instead?"

"No sale," said the nurse. "You're a guest here and you're going to be a polite guest and drink whatever the host serves."

She was as good as her word. In five minutes she returned with the two eggs and the tea on a brown plastic tray.

"Don't look so disappointed," she said, her plump cheeks dimpling. "I've brought you a dividend. Here."

She unfolded some newspapers that were under her arm and spread them on the bed. "You're quite a hero, Mr. Judson. And that cute little wife of yours couldn't be sweeter."

He picked up the *Examiner* and there on page one was a picture of Chally. It showed her in the rear of a church, kneeling between two pews, head bowed, eyes closed, praying. Minus all traces of make-up, her young face was pale with an expression of deep reverence, an expression almost Madonna-like in its tenderness and intensity. Beneath it was a caption: *Prays for Missing Test Pilot.*

Judson skipped through the article that told about the search for him. He turned to an inside page where there was an article about Chally, telling how she had gone alone to the church to pray for her husband, and including a number of paragraphs about her dancing career. Not all the facts were true, he noticed, especially those giving her credit for appearing in "several films" and ballets staged "in Pasadena and Beverly Hills."

He turned back to page one and looked at the photograph again.

"Isn't she just the sweetest thing?" said the nurse, looking over his shoulder. "When I saw that picture this morning I just about sat down and cried. You're very lucky to have a wife like that, Mr. Judson."

Judson nodded slowly. "I guess so. Has she——"

He paused because he didn't quite know how to phrase the question. "Has she been here to the hospital?"

"Not yet," said the nurse. "I imagine she was probably held up at the studios——you know how busy those little actresses are."

"Yes, of course," said Judson.

77

"There've been a lot of other people coming by, though."
The nurse ran a dust cloth across the metal foot of the bed.
"Your father waited most of the afternoon for you to wake
up and finally had to leave. He said he'd come again tonight.
The newspaper photographers have been waiting since this
afternoon, too. The doctor says it's up to you if you want
to be bothered by them."

"I don't want to see them," said Judson.

"I don't blame you," said the nurse. "I'll tell them to leave."

When she left, he leaned his head back against the cool
rungs of the bed and closed his eyes. Almost immediately he
began to think of his error in the J, the way he'd switched
on the emergency fuel system while she was at full throttle,
and he could feel his leg muscles tensing under the covers. He
tried to drive the thoughts from his mind, but the harder he
tried the worse they became, with sweat breaking out in his
armpits, and he was glad to see the nurse return because she
gave him something else to think about.

"They won't leave," she said. "They say if you'll give them
five minutes they can take the pictures and then they won't
bother you any more."

"Okay," said Judson, wearily. "I guess they've got a job to
do. Send them in."

"Not until you eat your eggs," she said. "You haven't
touched them."

"Okay," he said. "Okay."

Once while he cracked the shell on the first egg his unsteady
fingers dropped the spoon. He ate half the egg, his stomach
rebelling against the sulphurous yellow of the yolk, and sipped
a little of the tea which was weak and lukewarm.

"That's better," said the nurse. "I'll send them in."

The photographers, two men in sport jackets, entered the
room briskly and went right to work. Each posed him two
different ways, one standing on a chair for the particular angle
he needed, and when they departed after having used no more
than their predicted five minutes they left a group of black-
ened flashbulbs in the folds of the blankets.

"There's a Mr. Haynes to see you too," said the nurse.
"And a Mr. Spallanzani."

"Still no word from Mrs. Judson?" he asked.

78

She shook her head. "I'll let you know the moment she arrives. What about the others?"

"Send them in."

Spallanzani came first, boisterous as ever, bouncing on the bed to test the springs and making the usual cracks about where were all the pretty nurses. Haynes followed with a redhead on his arm, a tall girl in tight black slacks and a chartreuse bolero.

"They tell me that J turned into a blowtorch," grinned Spallanzani. "The old hot seat?"

Judson nodded. "The wick really lit."

"How was the ejection?" said Spallanzani. "Did I ever tell you about the—"

"Hold it a minute," said Haynes. He walked closer to the bed, leading the redhead by the hand. "Jud, I want you to meet somebody. She's been pestering me all day to meet you, ever since she saw your picture in one of the papers this morning." He turned to the girl. "Mimi, this is Jud. And Jud this is Mimi."

Judson gave her a mock salute. "Hello, Mimi."

"Hello yourself," she said. She smiled, revealing lower teeth that were tobacco stained. "I think you're just the most handsome man and when I saw your picture I said to myself I've just got to kiss that man."

She leaned over the bed and he caught a glimpse of the mascara on her lashes and the dark roots of her hair as her slick warm lips brushed his cheek.

"Hey, what's going on here?" demanded Haynes. "Didn't I tell you he's married?"

"No favorites," announced Mimi. "Although he's the most handsome, I never show favorites."

She kissed Spallanzani on the cheek and then kissed Haynes firmly on the mouth.

"Fair enough, boys?" she asked.

"Ah," sighed Haynes, closing his eyes, "if my wife could only pucker like that...."

"Haynes got more than I did," complained Spallanzani.

Shrugging, Mimi put her arms around his neck and kissed him long and hard on the lips.

"Better?" she said when they finished.

"My battery needle's twitching," said Spallanzani. Placing

his arm familiarly on her shoulder, he turned back to Judson. "Like I was saying before, about the ejection, you remember that fresh kid that came into the lounge one day claiming he'd been testing for Convair? The one with the white silk scarf around his neck and the gold wings on his Harris Tweed coat?"

"Yeah, I remember," said Judson. "Jack something his name was."

"That's the guy," said Spallanzani. "Well, I heard the other day he was ferrying an F-84 and had to eject when he threw a bucket. He was so scared he yanked his rip cord while he was still going up in the seat. The chute opened with him still sitting there in the seat. Well, when he finally got around to kicking out of the seat the damn thing went right up into the shrouds, got tangled somehow and stayed up there."

"A real jerk," said Haynes.

"You ain't heard the half of it," grinned Spallanzani."When he landed, the seat dropped from the shrouds, hit him on the head and knocked him colder than a sockeye salmon!"

Spallanzani slapped his thigh and laughed and Judson and Haynes joined in.

"Isn't he the same kid who ran out of fuel while flying a $100,000 entry to the Bendix races?" said Haynes. "Smashed it all to hell in a forced landing at Omaha. And I think—"

"Sorry, folks," interrupted the nurse. "Time's up. Mr. Judson needs his rest."

"He's resting," said Spallanzani. "He's flat on his back."

"Doctor's orders," said the nurse, leaving with the food tray. "I want you all to be gone when I get back in about one minute."

"Grouch," said Spallanzani, making a face at her as she went out. Then he drew closer to the bed, pulled a pint of Hill & Hill from the pocket of his coat and handed it to Judson. "Take a good pull, boy. You need it."

Judson nodded and tipped his head back. The whiskey was warm and smooth and peeled the boiled egg taste off his tongue. He lowered the level in the bottle half an inch before handing it back to Spallanzani.

"Thanks," he said.

"Want me to leave the bottle?" said Spallanzani.

Judson shook his head. "I'll be getting out pretty soon."

"You will not," said the nurse, returning. She took Spallanzani by the shoulders, turned him around and aimed him toward the door. "Now shoo, all of you."

"All right, all right," protested Spallanzani. "We're going. We'll be seeing you, Jud."

"So long," said Haynes, approaching the door.

"See you," said Judson. "Thanks for coming over."

"Goodbye, good-looking," said the redhead, waving. "Look me up sometime at the Bandbox on Fifth."

"Maybe I will," said Judson.

After they'd gone, the nurse fluffed up his pillows and emptied the ashtrays. Then she brought in the evening papers and some magazines and a pitcher of ice water.

"We still haven't heard from your little wife," she said. "I wonder what could be keeping her?"

"You know how busy those little actresses are," said Judson.

By the peculiar look the nurse gave him he saw that she did not understand the bitterness in his tone. He felt exremely tired and dropped back heavily against the pillows, still seeing the expression in Haynes' and Spallanzani's eyes. They'd tried. God knows they'd tried to keep the conversation light and easy but they couldn't conceal the expression, the fleeting behind-the-eyes expression which told better than words that they suspected there'd been another pilot error, that they suspected he'd lost his touch. He knew exactly how they felt because he'd felt the same way himself, standing awkwardly in the hospital room of some other pilot who'd washed one out, trying to keep things casual and humorous, trying to make the guy feel nothing had changed and knowing all the time the guy knew he was through.

"I thought I shooed you out of here," said the nurse.

Judson looked up as he heard footsteps coming into the room.

"Sorry, ma'm," said Spallanzani, "but I got to give my old buddy here the word."

"What's up?" said Judson.

"Don't get your tailpipe in an uproar," said Spallanzani. "Nothing serious. I just thought I better tell you Bixler's foaming at the mouth about what happened to the J, claiming Lansdale himself is sore about it. So Bixler'll probably chew you out from belly-button to appetite."

81

"I can take it," said Judson.

"Sure you can, Jud. I just wanted you to know I think Bixler's cracking up. I think his nerves are gone and he's bitching at us guys all the time trying to cover up. That's why I think he's going to fly the YF-188 himself. To show us he can do it—not because of what happened to you in the J."

Spallanzani got out his cigarette lighter, tested it unnecessarily a couple of times and replaced it in his pocket. His features were drawn and serious and the lines around his mouth looked old because the familiar grin was missing.

"Thanks," said Judson slowly. "Thanks a lot."

"Don't get me wrong," said Spallanzani. "There's no telling what that crazy Bixler may do. He may still pick you to fly the YF-188."

"But you don't really think so," said Judson.

"I didn't say that." Spallanzani hesitated and then started toward the door. "I got to get going because Haynes and the redhead are waiting—but there's one other thing I want to say, Jud."

Spallanzani got out his lighter again and fiddled with the flint.

"I don't know what happened up there in the J," he said, "and I don't want to know. All I know is that in my book you're the best test pilot that ever flew an airplane."

Spallanzani turned and went quickly out the door and down the hall.

The nurse dusted off the bureau top.

"My," she said, "he certainly thinks a lot of you."

Judson didn't reply. His throat felt suddenly dry and he poured himself a glass of ice water.

The nurse rearranged the room's two white, straightbacked chairs, tucked the blanket in at his feet and placed an ashtray on the nightstand where it would be in easy reach. Then she departed.

In a few minutes, she returned again, followed by his father and Dunc. His father wore a somber gray executive's suit with a dark blue tie while Dunc had on his new blue serge and his dark brown hair was brushed severely back. They came in on tiptoe, looking around strangely.

"For crying out loud," said Judson. "This isn't any funeral. Cheer up!"

"Glad to see you're all right, son," said his father, his palm cool and damp against Judson's as they shook hands.

"I'll be out of here in no time," said Judson.

"Was it—" His father revolved his hat in his hands. "Was it pretty bad?"

"Nothing to it," said Judson.

He lighted a cigarette and filled them in briefly on what had happened to the J, leaving out parts of the story which he knew would make the old man uneasy. Dunc remained at the foot of the bed, taking no part in the conversation but listening in that big-eyed way of his. Judson could see that the boy was still hurt and withdrawn because he hadn't been permitted to go to the plant and watch the test. As he talked about his night on the dinghy, he tried to think of something he could say to Dunc that would make him smile and join in. But nothing occurred to him except the model airplane and he wasn't sure even that subject was safe ground.

When he finished with his account of how the Coast Guard PBM had picked him up, there was a lull in the conversation and he decided to take the bull by the horns.

"How's the fuselage coming along, Dunc?" he asked.

"It's okay."

"How about the wing?"

"It's okay." The boy's blue eyes remained cool and aloof.

"You can talk about that when you get home." His father's voice took on its most pontifical tone. "Right now I've got something I'm going to say to you, Jud, something I've wanted to say for a long time. I want you to quit flying."

Picking up the ashtray, Judson crushed his cigarette hard against the plastic surface, extinguishing all the sparks, not looking up at his father.

"I know this isn't a subject you like to talk about," said his father. "But I can't hold back any longer. I want you to quit flying and take that job at the factory. I'll even make you vice president in charge of engineering and design for the new canning machinery I told you about."

Judson kept tamping the cigarette against the ashtray.

"Can't you even dignify my offer with a reply?" demanded his father. "And quit fooling around with that cigarette."

Judson put the ashtray on the nightstand.

"Dad," he said quietly. "You know how I feel."

"You never think about how I feel," said his father. "Or how your mother felt. And that's something else I'm going to tell you, something I never told you all these years because I figured you had enough on your mind. I always let you think it was having Dunc that killed your mother. Well, it wasn't. Not by a long shot. The thing that killed your mother was worrying about you after we got the War Department telegram that you'd been shot down over Germany. We had no idea then you were in the prison camp. She worried herself sick and after she had the baby she kept on worrying, losing weight, turning into a pale, weak little woman right before my eyes and all because of you and that crazy stubborn streak that made you join the Air Force and fly instead of the Army or the Navy."

His father stopped talking, turned abruptly away from the bed and went over to the window.

Chapter Eleven

"I—" Judson cleared his throat. He felt sick to his stomach again and he wished he'd accepted Spallanzani's offer to leave the bottle. "I'm sorry, Dad. I . . . . didn't realize."

His father remained at the window, keeping his back toward the bed. Dunc hung his head and looked down at the floor.

For a long interval none of them spoke.

Then his father turned around and Judson could see the tears glistening plainly in the corners of his eyes.

"You've got to quit flying, Jud." His father's voice was low and unsteady. "If you keep on, you're going to kill yourself—I don't know how you've lived this long all the chances you take."

"We don't take chances, Dad. We can't afford to. We—"

"Of course you take chances. How else could you test those killers you fly? And it's changing you. You're drinking too much, you're nervous and you're irritable and you can't get along with your wife—"

"Leave her out of it," said Judson.

"You can't leave her out of it." His father returned to the side of the bed. "She's part of it, just like we're all part of it, Dunc and me, too. Whatever you do affects all of us and that's why you've got to quit. You've got to...."

His father's voice trailed off and there was another silence in the room, a silence which wasn't broken until the nurse returned.

"Visiting hours are over, folks," she said. "You can come back tomorrow."

His father patted Judson on the shoulder. "Think it over, son. I'll be back tomorrow and we can talk about it some more."

"I'll think about it," said Judson.

He watched them go, Dunc still withdrawn and unfriendly, and then he rolled over, throwing the blankets across his shoulder with an angry trust of his hand.

"I just had a phone call from Mrs. Judson," said the nurse. "She's having a special rehearsal tonight at Madame somebody or other's. She says she'll be able to come tomorrow, though."

"Swell," said Judson. "I hope she trips and breaks her god damn neck."

The nurse looked at him with alarm. "What did you say, Mr. Judson?"

"You heard me," he said. "I'm nothing but a monster. And now if you'll kindly leave me alone I think I'll lay here and sulk for a few hours."

"Of course, Mr. Judson." The nurse pinched her lips together primly and swept out the door.

Not until noon the following day was Judson able to convince the doctors that he was well and rested enough to leave the hospital. Putting on his slacks and sport jacket which had been sent over from the hangar, he left shortly before visiting hours were to begin, glad he was escaping before the arrival of his father.

He boarded a Yellow cab at the hospital entrance-way and gave the driver Chally's address. After lying awake half the night thinking about the J and Chally and his mother, he'd made up his mind. He had to get things straightened out with Chally once and for all. He was sure now that it was all tied

85

in together—his uncertainty over her, his constant concern about her must be affecting his flying, making him forgetful, weakening his self-confidence. He had gone over the whole thing in his mind again and again, reviewing his past mistakes with her, promising himself that this time no matter what happened he would be gentle with her, gentle but persuasive.

He dismissed the taxi in front of the apartment house and went swiftly up the stairs to the fourth floor. He rang the doorbell several times before he noticed the small card with her name was missing from the brass frame on the door.

There was no answer. He returned to the lobby and talked to the woman at the desk and he had a feeling before the woman finished checking her list of tenants that Chally had moved again. The woman confirmed his suspicions and shook her head in reply to his questions. No, there had been no phone calls from Miss Falke since she'd left.

When he went back outside, he noticed a bar across the street, the Gyro Room, and he walked over to it. But when he got inside he decided bourbon wasn't what he wanted. He entered the phone booth at the rear and phoned Marjorie at the plant.

"Well, hello, Jud!" she said brightly. "How are you?"

"Fine," he said. "Full of fight."

"Are you still in the hospital?"

"Nope, just left. Too many lumps in the mattress."

"I was going to visit you last night," she said, "but I didn't want to interfere, what with Chally there and everybody else."

He hesitated and then decided there was no sense trying to keep the truth from her.

"She didn't show up," he said. "Rehearsing again, I guess."

"Well, I'll be darned!" Marjorie didn't attempt to conceal her anger. "The nerve of her. And after her picture was in all the papers, too. I hope you'll forgive me for saying this, Jud, but I think she just used the fact you were missing to cash in on a lot of free publicity. She's a lot smarter than—"

"Skip it, Marjorie," he said. "Maybe she had a good reason. Anyway, that isn't what I called you about. She's moved again and I was wondering if you'd give me the name of that friend of hers in personnel. Maybe she knows Chally's new address."

"Of course, Jud. And I'm sorry— I didn't mean to upset you by saying the wrong thing about Chally. She's very tal-

ented. I don't blame her a bit for wanting to be a success."
Marjorie paused. "Her friend's name is Lisa Robinsen. I can
give you her phone extension number if you want it."

"I think I better talk to her in person," said Judson. "And
thanks, Marjorie."

"You're welcome, Jud. When are you going to take me up
on that steak I've been saving for you in the refrigerator?"

"Soon," he said. "One of these days."

"Don't wait too long."

"Not a chance."

They talked for a few more moments and then he hung up
and left the bar. He hailed another Yellow cab and returned
to the plant, showing his badge to the security officer at the
gate, getting out in front of the super-modern administration
building and looking up as he always did at the enormous
metal replica of the world suspended over the main entrance.
He took the escalator to the mezzanine level and found Lisa
Robinsen working in a large office with a number of other
girls.

She was a small, natural blonde busily marking time cards
with a rubber stamp and she looked up as he approached her
desk. She wore a filmy white nylon blouse which plainly re-
vealed the straps of her slip and the shadowy V between the
cups of her bra.

"Hello, Lisa," said Judson, "I'm Chally's husband. Got a
minute?"

"Certainly."

Her blue eyes were the most intense he'd ever seen. They
were dark, nearly blue-black, with obscure depths that seemed
infinite, and he hesitated, almost forgetting why he'd come as
they surveyed him with a cool detachment.

"I was wondering," he said, "if you happen to know Chally's
new address."

She shook her head. "No, I'm afraid not."

"Have you seen her lately?"

"No."

"When was the last time you saw her?"

The expression in the blue-black eyes changed slightly and
he was certain he saw a flicker of contempt before the depths
closed in again, reassuming the expression of careful detachment. It occurred to him suddenly that Lisa knew about the

87

scene in the apartment when Chally had locked herself in the bedroom and the manager had kicked him out.

"I don't really remember the last time I saw her," said Lisa.

The vagueness of her reply stumped him and he couldn't think of any new questions.

"Are you sure you don't know her addess?" he repeated.

"Mr. Judson," she said icily, "I am not in the habit of lying."

"Sorry," he said. "I just thought Chally might have told you not to give it to me."

Picking up the rubber stamp, Lisa began marking the time cards again, her long-nailed hands moving with efficient speed.

"She did not," she said.

There was a finality in the way she said it that told him he was wasting his time. He said goodbye and left the office, trying to fathom her attitude as he rode down the escalator to the lobby. Her replies had been made with such an air of ease he had been sure at first she hadn't been lying. But there had also been an undercurrent of careful calculation which made each reply a little too perfect, a little too rehearsed to be truthful.

Under his breath he cursed Chally for covering her tracks so well. He ordered a cup of coffee in the company cafeteria and tried to think of some other way to run her down. But too many people—office brass, engineers and even riveters—recognized him and crowded around, insisting on the details of what had happened to the J, demanding to know how he had managed to cling all night to the dinghy.

He shook them off finally and left the building, boarding a plant bus which was leaving for the other end of the airport. As long as the bus was carrying him toward the test hangar, he decided he might as well get it over with—he might as well go in and face Bixler.

When he entered the hangar and walked past a J which was being worked on by two crew chiefs, he felt the tenseness—the now familiar tenseness—return to his belly. There was something so god damned deadly about the angle of the swept-back wing, something so efficiently superhuman about it that he didn't want to look at it any more. He averted his eyes, angry with himself for such weakness, and went up the metail stairs to the lounge.

They were all there—Spallanzani, White, Haynes and Bixler —and he was thankful for their casualness. They greeted him and then kept right on talking about red-out, with White arguing that a man couldn't stand continual total red-out for more than seven seconds and Haynes and Spallanzani arguing that five was the limit.

"What about you, Jud?" said Haynes. "You got any opinions?"

"I'd say no more than five seconds," said Judson. "Anyway who ever heard of an airplane that could produce more than five or six seconds of red-out?"

"Right," said Spallanzani, "and I hope to hell they never build one."

Bixler got up from his leather chair and stretched lazily and although the men continued talking they glanced at him and then at Judson.

"Got a few minutes, Jud?" said Bixler. "I want to talk to you." He gestured at the hall. "Out there."

Judson nodded. He followed Bixler through the door and closed it carefully behind him.

"I played back the tape Obdorsk made on the J," said Bixler, "and there are a few things I want to ask you."

Bixler got out a pack of cigarettes and put one in his mouth without offering one to Judson.

"You lost your fuel pressure?" said Bixler.

Judson nodded.

"Switched to your emergency system?"

"Yes," said Judson.

"That's when she started to overheat?" Bixler's mouth twisted crookedly. "Right after that?"

"Just about then," said Judson, knowing what Bixler was getting at.

Bixler folded his arms across his chest, rubbing the knuckle of his right thumb with his forefinger.

"You sure you retarded the throttle to idle before you switched on the emergency?" said Bixler.

"Of course," said Judson. It was a lie that he did not feel guilty about it.

"You sure?"

Judson wished Bixler would quit rubbing his forefinger so nervously across his knuckle.

89

"Of course I'm sure," said Judson. "It's elementary. Nobody ever switches on the emergency without throttling first to idle."

"Then why did she overheat?"

"Damned if I know. It could have been any number of things. She'd been giving the mechanics fits all day."

He noticed that there was a large horny callus on Bixler's thumb and it occurred to him that Bixler must've been rubbing on for months.

"The YF-188 gets her first test tomorrow," said Bixler, "and I might as well tell you right now you won't be flying her."

He made the statement coldly, his eyes hard and satisfied, and Judson felt a flash of anger.

"Why not?" said Judson.

"You already know why."

"Why?" demanded Judson. "Quit beating around the bush!"

"You want the truth?" Bixler's voice was beaded with sarcasm. "Then I'll give you the truth. Your nerves are shot. You think I'd trust you with a couple of million dollars worth of prototype? You're so tense you couldn't fly your way out of a wet paper bag. And besides that you're a god damn liar."

Judson felt his hands clenching and unclenching at his sides.

"What did you call me?" he said.

"I'm calling you a liar because I think you forgot to throttle to idle." With an abrupt gesture, Bixler threw his cigarette to the floor. "And I'm calling you a liar because you're not man enough to admit it!"

Judson swung. And as his fist traveled in an arc, he saw a glint in Bixler's eye that told him Bixler was glad the open rebellion he'd been waiting for day after day was finally occurring. But Judson didn't care whether he got fired or not. He put his weight behind the blow and scored a direct hit on Bixler's cheekbone, the contact of bone against bone sending shock waves up his arm. Bixler reeled backwards and Judson hit him again, in the mouth this time, feeling his anger running away with him and exhilarating in it. Bixler's shoulders slammed into the door, opening it and he stumbled backward into the lounge, bringing the other men in a rush from their chairs.

Judson swung again, missed, and took a punch in the throat from Bixler who had found his balance. Judson hit him in the eye and then he felt a terrific smash in his belly and he couldn't

90

understand how Bixler had managed to hit him there. Roaring with pain, he hurled himself at Bixler, both fists flying, and then he felt himself being caught from behind.

Strong arms held him back and at the same time Haynes and White closed in on Bixler, holding him back also.

"Let go!" Judson wrestled and tried to free himself.

"You silly bastard!" Spallanzani hissed in his ear. "You'll get yourself canned!"

"God damn it, let me go!" Judson twisted around, shoved Spallanzani in the chest and broke loose.

He stormed toward Bixler, but Haynes intercepted him, pinning his arms to his sides, and then Spallanzani got a new grip on him and the two men led him over to the leather divan and sat him down hard upon it.

For a long moment, the room was quiet except for the heavy sounds of Judson's and Bixler's breathing.

Bixler stepped away from White, wiped his fingers across his mouth and they came away bloody. He looked at them and then he looked at Judson, his eyes narrow and shiny, his face pale.

"This tears it!" he said.

He turned and went out the door, the leather heels of his flight boots striking hard against the floor of the hallway, the sounds diminishing as he reached the end of the hallway and went down the stairs.

Chapter Twelve

JUDSON TURNED ANGRILY to Spallanzani. "Why'd you stop me? I wanted to beat the living hell out of him!"

"Sure," said Spallanzani, "and we don't blame you a bit, but for Christ's sake you want to get yourself fired?"

"There are other jobs," said Judson. "I don't have to take his crap!"

"Simmer down, Jud." Haynes touched his shoulder. "I don't

91

think he'll fire you. He'd have to explain the whole thing to the brass and he can't afford to do that because they wouldn't have any respect for him if they found out he'd been brawling with one of his own men. Anyway, you got the satisfaction of pasting him a few."

"Yeah," said White. "I've been wanting to take him on all week myself."

"What started it?" asked Spallanzani.

"He told me I wasn't going to fly the YF-188." Rubbing his knuckles where the skin was torn, Judson got up from the divan. "One thing led to another."

"Why the lousy weasel!" said White. "He knows damn well it's your turn to collect a $4000 bonus. He collected the last one."

Judson shrugged. "He's the boss."

"He's a lousy boss," said White. "Throwing his weight around like a top sergeant. He used to be bad enough but the last couple of weeks have really been the end."

"Must be the YF-188 that's worrying him," said Spallanzani. "That baby's going to be fast, awful damned fast."

"Too fast," said White. "I think she's too—"

White flushed suddenly, realizing he'd said too much, realizing he'd stepped across the invisible line that they all knew was there and so carefully avoided.

An awkward silence filled the room.

"What I mean is—" White hesitated. "I mean I don't think Bixler should fly the YF-188. I don't think he's in shape for it. I think you should take her up, Jud."

"He's right, Jud," said Haynes. "Not only because it's your turn to collect, but because you're a better pilot than Bixler. I think you better have it out with him again and tell him you've got to fly the YF-188."

"I don't want to talk to him," said Judson.

He kept his voice restrained as if it were the most natural thing in the world for him to be talking about flying the YF-188, as if he really wanted to do the test. But inside he was incredulous. It didn't seem possible that all three of them —Spallanzani, Haynes and White—didn't suspect what had happened up in the J. It wasn't reasonable that Bixler was the only one who suspected what had happened. He looked at their faces and wondered if they were pretending they didn't know just to give him confidence in facing Bixler.

"What can you lose?" said Spallanzani.

"I saw him get in his car after he left here," said White. "If I know Bixler he's probably over at Ditman's."

"Okay, okay," said Judson. "I'll go find him but I don't think it'll do any good."

He left the lounge, walked across the floor of the hangar and out to the parking lot where he got into the Buick. As he drove out the security gate, the incongruity of the situation disturbed him, making him disgusted with himself. He didn't want to fly the YF-188. He didn't want to be anywhere near it when the chocks were pulled, yet here he was calmly driving to see Bixler.

He found Bixler at the far end of the bar at Ditman's, a double scotch in his hand and a fine purple mouse beginning to appear under his left eye.

Sitting down on the adjacent stool, Judson ordered a bourbon and water from Hugo.

"What're you doing here?" grunted Bixler. "You want your block knocked off?"

"If you think you're big enough to do it," said Judson. "I didn't come here to apologize, that's for sure. You deserved what you got."

Bixler set his glass down hard and turned quickly on his stool, his jaw thrusting out. "Watch what you're saying, Jud, I'm warning you!"

"Can it," said Jud, "and listen to me. I'll admit I made a mistake in the J. I didn't throttle down before switching on the emergency fuel system. It was one of those things, a mistake anybody can make and nine times out of ten it can be corrected quick enough so there's no trouble."

"And what about what happened out on the runway the other day?" said Bixler. "You smashed hell out of that 160K's strut."

"Accidents can happen. I was—"

"That was a dumb pilot's error," said Bixler, "the kind a pilot like you shouldn't make in a million years. You've lost your touch, Jud."

"You're crazy!" said Judson, but he could feel a lack of conviction in his words. He lifted the glass Hugo set before

93

him and downed a fourth of it. "I can still fly circles or squares around you, gear up or gear down, and you know it. The YF-188 job should be mine and god damn it, Bixler, I don't think you've got the right to beat me out of it!"

Bixler turned and jabbed Judson slowly and deliberately in the chest with his stubby forefinger.

"A couple of weeks ago you could fly circles around me, Jud, but no more. I'm not assigning the YF-188 job to you and I'm not assigning it to Haynes or White or Spallanzani either because they're not up to that baby. I'm assigning it to myself because I'm the only one in the bunch I can trust. And that's that."

He picked up his glass, tilted his head back and drained what was left of the scotch.

"That's $4000 you're beating me out of," said Judson. "I don't like it."

"Here's something else you're not going to like," said Bixler. "You're grounded."

"What?"

"You heard me, Jud." Bixler's mouth was a thin, uneven line. "You're not setting foot in even a 160K. Until I give the word you stay on the ground, understand?"

Judson slid off his stool. "Why you son of a —"

"It's for your own damn good!" said Bixler.

He slid from his stool and they stood there toe to toe, so close Judson could see the webbing of deep, premature lines around Bixler's eyes.

"You're nothing but a hazard to yourself and the rest of us," said Bixler. "Why don't you admit it?"

Judson started to reply and then thought better of it. Because Bixler was right. He was a hazard. Like an airplane with a short circuit in its wiring, or water in its fuel, he wasn't safe to take into the air.

Without another word, he turned, walked away from the bar and went out the door.

He didn't get home until after midnight. The house was gloomy and silent as he went unsteadily up the stairs and along the hallway. When he passed Dunc's room, he heard the springs of the boy's bed creak and he opened the door. After

94

fumbling along the wall, he found the light switch and flipped it.

"H'lo, Dunc," he said. "How're y'doin'?"

Dunc sat up and looked at him, blinking against the brightness of the light.

"You're stewed again," said Dunc.

He rolled over and turned his face to the wall.

"Aw, that's no way to treat an ol' buddy," said Judson. "C'mon, turn around."

But the boy didn't move, his body making a slim rigid mound under the blankets and yellow and white striped bedspread.

"Okay, okay," said Judson. "I can take a hint."

He put out the light and went along the hall to his own room. Slipping out of his slacks and shirt, he left his underwear on, fell into the bed and dragged the covers over his shoulders.

He went to sleep immediately, and it was a deep almost drugged sleep without dreams or nightmares. But nevertheless at dawn he awoke with the clanks, his legs and body shaking, the sheets soaked with a cold sweat. He tried to sit up but his head ached and he dropped back against the pillow, holding his knees in an effort to make them stop shaking. It seemed to take the clanks longer to pass this time and when he was finally able to sit up and light a cigarette, he was weak and sick to his stomach. He stayed in one position a long time, arms folded, knees pressing almost against his chest, and didn't move until he heard Opal stirring down in the kitchen.

After he heard his father go downstairs, followed a little later by Dunc, he got up and put on his wrinkled slacks and shirt. He didn't feel like shaving. He went down the stairs slowly, pausing in the hallway when he heard his father and Dunc talking about him exactly as they had talked about him on previous mornings. Without hesitation Dunc parried his father's questions and told him no, Jud hadn't been drunk when he came home.

Judson went into the kitchen, took a cup of steaming coffee from Opal and apologized to his father for not being at the hospital the previous afternoon. He tried to catch Dunc's eye to let him know he was grateful for the way he had covered

95

up for him, but the boy kept his eyes carefully averted as he ate his Cream of Wheat.

Not until after their father left did Dunc speak again. As he went out the door, schoolbooks under his arm, he looked back at Judson accusingly.

"The shop man brought the Jag home yesterday," he said. "He told me you wrecked it."

"He did?" Judson set his cup down in the drops of spilled coffee on the saucer.

"Why did you tell me you loaned it to one of the guys?" said Dunc. His blue eyes were confused and hurt.

"I don't know," said Judson slowly. "I honestly don't know. I—"

But the rest of his reply was lost as Dunc slammed the door and ran down the walk.

Judson remained in his chair, drinking several cups of coffee, waving away the dish of eggs and bacon that Opal wanted to set before him. He tried to think of some way to square himself with Dunc, but nothing occurred to him. That was the trouble with a kid like Dunc. He was different than other kids. He couldn't be bribed with a new toy or some candy bars because in many ways he was as mature as any grown-up.

"Aren't you going to shave today?" asked Opal, clearing away the dishes.

"No," he said.

He went into the living room and picked up the morning paper but he couldn't concentrate on it. When the grandfather clock in the hall struck eight with its flat, unmusical tone he knew Bixler was taxiing the YF-188 by now and might even, if she felt right, be taking her up. He tossed the papers aside, went upstairs and took a shower and shaved. Then, in a clean brown and white figured sport shirt and his green slacks, he walked a few blocks to the drugstore on Wyatt Street, bought a carton of cigarettes and returned home.

At ten o'clock, he couldn't wait any longer. Phoning the plant, he talked to White in the lounge.

"Any word from Edwards on the YF-188?" he asked.

"They're not going to test her till tomorrow," said White. "They're installing a new kind of actuating cylinder that's taking longer than they figured." He paused. "Say, Jud, we're all plenty sore around here at the way Bixler grounded you. He had no right to do that."

"He's the boss," said Judson.

"Go over his head," said White. "Go see Lansdale himself."

"Maybe I will in a couple of days if Bixler doesn't change his mind."

"I wouldn't wait," said White.

They hung up and Judson went back upstairs to his room. He killed an hour rearranging the calculus and engineering volumes in the twin bookcases beside his bed, something he'd been intending to do for months. When he was nearly finished, two books fell from a pile he was carrying, falling open on the floor. He picked them up, noticing the corner of an envelope protruding from the leaves of one. He took out the envelope and turned it over slowly in his hands.

It was the first note Chally had ever written him. He'd received it after their first date and as he opened it and re-read it he was surprised that it had been written only four months before. It seemed so much longer than that.

He read the words again, admiring her rounded, backslanting script on the peach-colored stationary.

"Dear Jud: I had a wonderful time. And I certainly would love to see you fly sometime. All my best, Chally."

Quite suddenly he remembered the first time he'd seen her. It had been in the administration building, near her office in personnel, and she'd been bending over the drinking fountain. When she raised up, the pink tip of her tongue brushing the droplets of water from her lips, she looked at him and smiled and he felt himself go all warm inside. She was so very young, so clear-eyed and so casual. He didn't remember how he started the conversation but he kept her there for at least half an hour, talking about trivialities, laughing, and when she left he had a promise for a date the next Friday night.

He folded the note carefully and replaced it in its peach-colored envelope, remembering that first date and the details of the others that had followed in rapid order. Love at first sight. And nearly as wonderful had been the fact that she was genuinely interested in his flying and not afraid of it.

He put the letter back in the book but his hand paused in mid-air as he set it back on the shelf because another thought occurred to him. She had said she wasn't afraid of his flying—

but maybe she'd said it in an effort to do the right thing, in order to put him at his ease with her. She had said the same thing a few more times after that and then for a long time the subject hadn't come up again. He wondered if secretly she was afraid of his flying, like the wives of the other test pilots. Maybe that was what was wrong with their marriage. Maybe she was afraid all the time, worrying about him.

He swore and with his fist rammed the books up against the back of the bookcase. If he could just find her again and talk things over.

Throwing himself on the bed, he put his hands behind his neck and looked up at the ceiling, noticing the mark that was still there in the plaster from the time he and Dunc crashed one of Dunc's gliders against it. And then, out of the blue, he remembered that he'd never checked whether or not there actually was a Madame Broquet's.

He went to the extension phone on the nightstand in his father's bedroom and thumbed through the phone book. And it was there *Madame Francine Broquet's School of the Ballet.*

Immediately, he picked up the phone and began to dial.

But he hung up before he finished, realizing that Chally had undoubtedly told people at the school not to give her address to her husband. He thought a moment, recalling she had mentioned that a choreographer from MGM had offered her an audition.

Again he dialed. A secretary answered and he asked to speak to Madame Broquet.

In a moment a feminine voice with a soft French accent came on the line.

"Good morning," said Judson, "this is MGM calling and we'd like some additional information on Miss Charlotte Falke for our files."

"Of course, of course," trilled Madame Broquet. "You must be Monsieur Walton."

"Yes, I am," said Judson. "We need to know Miss Falke's height, weight and—" He paused, trying to think of some other statistic a studio might require.

"Hair coloring, lipstick, bra size—the usual?" said Madame Broquet.

"Yes," said Judson, "the usual."

When she gave him the information, he pretended to copy it down.

"Home address and phone number?" he asked.

"Let me see. . . ." Madame Broquet paused. "She's moved so much recently. Oh, here it is—2241 Gripsholm Place. I'm sorry, but we don't have her new phone number."

"That's all right," Judson said. "I'll get it another time. And now may I speak to Miss Falke if she isn't busy in a class?"

"She isn't here." A note of concern crept into Madame Broquet's tone. "She hasn't been here all week. I assumed she was at the studio."

"Of course," said Judson, "I should have remembered. I'm sure she's over at our rehearsal studios. I'll have her phone you. And thank you for the information, Madame Broquet."

"You're welcome, Monsieur Walton. And I do hope you'll come out to the school again. We have a Madamoiselle Dubrulle who has a stunning figure and I'm sure if you see her you'll—"

"Yes, of course," said Judson. "I'll be out again one of these days. Goodbye, Madame Broquet."

He hung up, tore off the sheet on which he'd copied the address, strode to his room and got his coat.

Chapter Thirteen

HE PRESSED the doorbell button several more times and still there was no answer. Going downstairs, he checked with the elevator man and received directions to the building superintendent's office. After arguing several minutes and displaying the picture of Chally in his wallet, he convinced the building superintendent that he was her husband and the elderly man grudgingly took him back upstairs and let him into the apartment.

When the building superintendent departed, Judson glanced around the living room, astonished at the mess it was in. The white leather suitcases he'd given Chally for a honeymoon present were piled on a chair, some open, some closed. An armload of dresses was thrown in a rainbow-like spray across the back of another chair. A cardboard box filled with ballet slippers stood on one of the blonde, hardwood end tables. Half a dozen dirty glasses were on the mantel along with two empty whiskey bottles. The ashtrays were filled with cigarette butts, most of them stained with lipstick.

He went into the small kitchen, found the sink piled with dirty dishes and one of the faucets dripping. A saucepan of garbage stood beside a pile of canned vegetables and some wilted celery and heads of lettuce which had not been placed in the refrigerator. The bedroom was just as bad—bed unmade, nylon stockings on the white shag rug, a housecoat tossed across the collection of lotions and creams on the dressing table.

Reluctantly, but feeling he must, he hunted for male signs —a necktie, cigar butt or cardboard stiffeners from a freshly-laundered shirt. He found none and, relieved, returned to the living room.

It was a long afternoon. He watched television and when that grew boring turned on the radio. Again and again when he heard footsteps in the hall, he thought it was Chally returning and each time he was disappointed.

When it grew twilight, he began to pace the floor, smoking cigarette after cigarette and rubbing his hands together. He went out to the kitchen and found a bottle of scotch in one of the cabinets over the sink. There were only two inches of liquor in it. He poured the liquid in a glass and drank it quickly, feeling the warmth of it but no other effect except hunger. He fixed himself some canned split pea soup, heating it in a pan on the stove, and ate it with some crackers.

Seven o'clock passed. Then eight o'clock. He dialed MGM, and asked if a late rehearsal were being held, but the switchboard operator said she didn't know because the studio offices had closed at five.

When it was nearly midnight, he left, tired and aching for a drink, his nerves taut as cello strings.

He drove straight to Ditman's and ordered a double bourbon, drank half of it in two long gulps and then looked around the dim room. Spallanzani and Mimi, the redhead who'd visited him at the hospital, were crowded together, arms entwined, in one of the large green-leather booths. Haynes and White were in another booth, talking with Marjorie, and when she noticed him she got up and came over to the bar.

. "Hello, Jud," she said. "I was hoping you'd come in."

"Hello," he said.

"Something wrong?" she asked, sliding onto the next stool.

"Nothing," he said. "Everything."

"Care to talk about it? I'm a great little listener and my fees are reasonable."

He turned and looked at her. She wore a scarlet gabardine coat with large velvet black buttons and her shining blonde hair was upswept into curls held in place with amber-jeweled barrettes.

"What are you drinking?" he said.

"I've had enough," she said. "Thanks anyway. Sure you wouldn't like to talk about it?"

"I don't think so," he said.

She put her elbow on the bar, propped her hand under her chin and looked up at him. "Well, what shall we talk about then?"

"I don't know." He shrugged. "Tell me about when you were a little girl."

"How little?" she asked. "Tea party and mud pies little or would you prefer when I was a teen-ager?"

"A teen-ager," he said. "I've always wondered what goes on in those wise young female minds."

"Well...." Marjorie paused. "I could tell you about when I was fifteen. I fell in love with the boy who lived across the street. I believe it was—yes, I'm sure it was exactly two days after I got my first permanent."

"And I suppose it was a beautiful affair," he said. "Hand-holding in the park, sodas at the five and ten, rubbing knees at the movie."

"Yes—and at the end we rode off together into the sunset on his bicycle." Marjorie laughed. "Actually, it wasn't like that at all."

"No hand-holding?"

"None," she said. "He used to water his folks' lawn in the evening, so then I would get our hose and water our lawn at the same time. And we just stood there not saying a word, not

101

even hello, and he never even looked over at me. He took great pains to keep his eyes on the grass he was watering."

"So then what happened?"

"That was it. We watered our lawns at the same time every night, standing on our separate sidewalks, acting as if the other one wasn't there at all. And I can remember how I used to look forward to it for hours because I was very much in love with him, you know. It had a tragic ending."

"He turned the hose on you one night?" said Judson.

Marjorie's dark blue eyes twinkled as she smiled. "No. His family moved away and I never saw him again."

"But it turned out all right," said Judson. "Ten years later, when you were both all nicely grown up, you met on a bus and this time he talked a blue streak and you were married the next day. So it proves that—"

He halted because at the word marriage Marjorie's face had changed and he realized he'd said the wrong thing.

"No, I married George," she said quietly. "And I've—"

"I'm sorry, Marjorie." He reached out and covered her smooth hand with his. "I didn't intend to make you remember."

"It's all right." She smiled, a little too brightly. "I'm completely over it, you know. But what I was leading up to tell you is that you—with your good shoulders and dark hair and the way you swing your legs when you walk—you quite often remind me of that boy across the street."

"Even with these lines around my eyes?" he said. "And all these gray ones?" He touched the hair at his temple.

"They're premature and don't count," she said. "Besides, it's attitude that's important and despite the long face you've been wearing these last few weeks I think you're still the youngest thirty-year-old I've ever met."

"Thirty-one," he said. "Thirty-two in a couple of months."

"What difference does it make?" she asked.

"A lot," he said. His glass was empty and he signalled the bartender.

"Don't," she said.

"Don't what?"

"Don't order another drink." Gently, her fingers touched the sleeve of his coat. "May I be candid with you, Jud?"

"I like you best when you're candid."

"Then I will be," she smiled. "Have I mentioned lately that I've still got those two steaks in my refrigerator?"

He looked into her eyes and saw that she was serious.

"You realize it's past twelve-thirty?" he said.

"Certainly."

"Why you son-of-a-gun," he said. "What are we waiting for?"

He dropped a dollar bill on the bar, took her arm and they went out to the Jaguar. She sat close to him on the short ride to her small house at Playa del Rey on the west side of the airport. When they went in the front door, she switched on the lights in the living room and kitchen and removed her scarlet coat.

"Take your coat off, too," she said. "You might as well be comfortable while you wait. I'll try to be quick."

She was better than her promise. In twenty minutes, while he stood in the doorway trying to keep out of her way, she prepared hash browned potatoes, mixed a green salad and fried two top sirloins on the stainless steel grill on her electric range. While they ate at the small drop-leaf table under the kitchen windows, he found himself admiring the way the cloth of the sleeveless white dress, with its simple pattern of tiny black clubs and spades, fitted tautly—with small emphasizing folds— across the rounded surfaces of her breasts.

"What are you looking at?" she asked.

"You," he said. "I never realized what a good cook you are."

"But you're not looking at the food," she said.

"I don't have to in order to taste it," he said. "A nice arrangement in view of the excellent scenery around here."

"Such as the pans in the sink and the chipped paint on the breadbox?" she said.

"No," he said, "I'm talking about the blonde across the table with the hell of a good-looking figure."

"I thought you were concentrating on the food," she said.

"Food?" he said. "What food?"

Placing his knife and fork across his plate, he pushed his chair back and went around to her side of the table. He pulled her chair back.

"But I'm not through yet," she protested.

"You're through," he said.

"Why, Jud," she said, standing up, "I had no idea you were the Cro-Magnon type. I thought—"

He kissed her and she came swiftly into his arms, her hands tight and warm against his neck and he could smell the gardenia fragrance of her yellow hair. He kissed her a second time and her lips parted and he could feel the firm straightness of her teeth and taste the utter softness of her mouth.

He ran his fingers through her curls, grasped a handful and pulled gently until her head tilted back and their lips separated slowly.

"You're murder, Marjorie," he said. "Plain murder!"

She didn't reply. Closing her eyes, she leaned her head on his shoulder, rubbing her smooth forehead against his cheek and then she turned suddenly and kissed him hard and he reacted in the only possible way.

When he heard the jangling sound, he thought it was the alarm clock in his father's room. Then gradually he realized that this sound was different because it was coming in abrupt, ringing intervals.

"It's for you, Jud," somebody said.

He opened one eye and saw that he was in the bedroom and a girl was standing beside the nightstand, holding the phone out to him. For a second he thought it was Chally and then with a rush of memory he realized it was Marjorie. She wore a short, hip-length nightgown of sheer blue nylon, a length which accentuated the slim long lines of her legs.

She spoke again. "It's for you, Jud."

He took the phone, still half-asleep. "For me?"

"Yeah, for you," said Spallanzani when he put the phone against his ear. "Get out of that sack!"

"Why should I?" said Judson.

"Snap to it," said Spallanzani. "Bixler's changed his mind. You're off the grounded list, as of right now. You've got a target run at Edwards in exactly thirty minutes!"

"Okay, okay, I'll be there." Judson paused. "How in the hell did you know where I was?"

Spallanzani laughed. "Saw you leave Ditman's with her last night and I put two and two together. Which reminds me— how did you manage it? The rest of us have been trying to

104

score there for months and we got the cold shoulder before our trottles were halfway open."

"Go peddle your papers," said Judson. "I'll be right over."

He handed the phone back to Marjorie.

"Do you have to go?" she asked.

"Afraid so," he said. "What time is it?"

She picked her wrist watch up from the bureau top. "Eight-thirty."

"That late?" He yawned and stretched. "I haven't slept this late for weeks."

"There are some shaving things in the bathroom," she said. "They're George's—I never got around to putting them away."

"Thanks," he said, throwing the covers aside.

She went out the bedroom door, shutting it behind her, and he slipped into his slacks and shoes and walked into the bathroom. Finding a tube of brushless cream in the medicine cabinet, he lathered his face and then shaved with a worn safety razor which was surprisingly easy on his face. He felt rested and calm but at the same time uneasy about standing in front of George's mirror, rinsing George's razor in hot water from a faucet that George had undoubtedly used many, many times.

When he put on his coat in the living room, Marjorie came in from the kitchen with a steaming cup of coffee. Standing there drinking it, he felt her eyes watching him and he had a feeling of awkwardness because what had seemed right the night before seemed to be so absolutely wrong when examined in the cool gray light of morning.

"I think I ought to apologize," he said. "Last night I had no intention of—"

She laid a gentle finger on his lips.

"Shush," she said. "There's nothing to apologize for."

"I think I should," he said. "I didn't—"

"I led you on," she interrupted. "Quite shamelessly from the time I met you at Ditman's right on down the line."

"Why did you do it?"

"Because I wanted to, Jud. Because I felt it was something. ... " She stepped closer and kissed him softly at the side of his mouth. "Something we both needed. ... I've only got one regret—I hope you don't think I'm cheap."

"Far from it," he said. "You—"

105

"No more speeches," she smiled. "You better get to the plant before you're late."

"Right," he said.

He set the empty coffee cup on the glass top of the bookcase and opened the front door. When he was out on the small porch, he looked back at her.

"So long, Marjorie," he said. "You were murder....."

Then he walked rapidly out to the gray Jaguar at the curb.

.

Chapter Fourteen

THE FEELING of bouyancy left him as he drove down Imperial Boulevard and thought about flying again and how he had cheated on Chally. An F-160K took off with a roar, leaping upward on a path which paralleled the boulevard, and his hands tightened on the steering wheel and he felt the familiar contractions in his throat.

The tenseness stayed with him after he parked and went into the supply office at the hangar and signed for a new parachute and a white plastic helmet. He never liked new gear. It always felt stiff and alien. He stowed both items at the dispatch office and then went up to lounge. It was deserted, but on one of the desks were a test card with his name on it and a note from Spallanzani saying he'd see him at the north base at Edwards.

He read over the card, swearing when he saw that he would be flying another J, running a firing test at a towed sleeve. A memo on the card said the J would be outfitted with rockets at Edwards.

He jerked back nervously as the inter-com rasped into action at his elbow.

"Jud there?" said the dispatcher.

Judson depressed the button. "I'm here."

"Your J's waiting on the apron."

"Okay," said Jud. "I'll be there in five minutes."

He went into the locker room, removed his slacks and slipped into his G-suit. As he transferred his wallet, comb and other incidentals to the G-suit pockets, he came across the large, golden earring which Chally had dropped that other morning in the Buick. He turned it over in his fingers, thinking about her with a deep sense of guilt, which he couldn't shake off, and then he stuffed it quickly in his pocket, slammed the locker door and went outside.

As he approached the airplane, feeling the cold perspiration beginning to gather at his temples under the helmet, he had an abrupt sensation of nausea in his stomach. It was a fierce nausea, worse even than he'd felt during the long night on the raft, and the suddenness of it left him gasping. He leaned against the wing slats, his vision swimming and a brackish taste flooding his mouth.

The crew chief came around from the other side of the fuselage and Judson straightened up.

"Something the matter?" said the crew chief.

"No," said Judson. He swallowed some of the excess saliva. "Where's Eddie?"

"He's still working on the YF-188 at Edwards."

"That's right," said Judson. "I forgot."

He decided his legs were much too unsteady for the exterior walk-around check. Adjusting the straps on his chute, he went up the yellow ladder, sat down in the cockpit and handed the ejection safety pins to the crew chief. For the next five minutes, while the crew chief busied himself with the power cart back toward the tail, Judson sat there staring numbly at the instruments, fighting down an overpowering desire to vomit, wondering if he had the nerve to walk back to the hangar and tell them he'd do the test some other time.

The crew chief came back up the ladder, wiping a yellowish spot of oil from his cheek.

"Ready?" he asked.

Judson shook his head.

"You sure there ain't something wrong?" asked the crew chief.

"No, damn it!" said Judson, more harshly than he'd intended. "I'll let you know when I'm ready!"

The crew chief shrugged and went back down the ladder.

Very slowly, checking each item off twice, Judson went over the cockpit check-offs. Five more minutes passed, then ten, and he could tell by the crew chief's glances that he was growing more curious.

He shoved the engine master switch to "on" and cranked her up. As soon as he had 3 per cent rpm, he moved the throttle outboard and engaged the fuel booster pumps. Still working slowly, he completed the rest of the starting procedures, his eyes watching the tailpipe temperature needle tilt up into the green and then into the red. He waited for ignition—three seconds, four seconds, five and then six—saw that it was a false start, closed the throttle and hit the stop-start switch.

While he waited for the excess fuel to drain, he removed his leather gloves and wiped his sweaty palms against his trouser legs. Then he went through the starting steps a second time and again he failed to get ignition.

It was enough. He'd seen men leave airplanes on flimsier excuses than this. Unfastening his safety harnesses, he stood up in the cockpit.

Quickly, the crew chief came up the ladder. "Something wrong?"

Judson couldn't face the probing expression in the man's eyes. He sat down and refastened the straps.

"Nothing wrong," he said. His voice had a noticeable break. "Just wanted to. . . . stretch my legs."

Again he went through the starting steps, gaining ignition this time and feeling his stomach ball up as the engine roared, making the backrest behind him and the consoles beside him vibrate at a high rough pitch. He completed the remainder of the procedures, signalled for the power cart to be disconnected and the chocks pulled and then he taxied out onto the strip.

When he was poised at the end of the runway, the engine winding at a shrieking, deafening 100 per cent, the fear within him was so tremendous it was almost as if there were two men, two selves, in the cockpit—the man who couldn't fly and the man who had to. He released the brakes and the J rushed down the runway.

His hands were awkward and heavy on the controls and his

108

teeth were locked together so hard he could feel the pressure all the way to his brain. He found it impossible to believe that he was the same person who had effortlessly lifted airplane after airplane from this same runway. Because the J wouldn't life. It rolled and it rolled and it rolled—1300 feet, 1500 feet, 1800—and then he realized that although he thought he had been easing back slightly on the stick he actually hadn't been.

He got the stick back and the J horsed into the air, the starboard wingtip tipping dangerously close to the deck before he straightened her out. He raised the gear and flaps, saw that all the locks were normal, and pushed on up to 15,000. The feeling of clumsiness, the loss of touch on the stick stayed with him during the entire ten minutes of the ninety-mile trip to the desert. And the nausea and the strain on his nerves grew worse as he banked over Edwards, blinking as the full glare of the hot sun mirrored up at him from the miles of flat, hard-packed sand.

The north base tower gave him permission to come in and he set her down fast on the long diagonal runway, double-checking every move in the cockpit with a stiff concentration that made his head ache. It was not a good landing. The J bounced hard, tires protesting with a brief, animal-like squeal, and the nose wheel settled to the swift-running surface sooner than it should have. He taxied off the runway past a row of heavy bombers and then past a crew of men working on Lockheed's tall vertical riser. He parked between two 160Ks, pulled on the parking brakes and let the engine idle for a couple of minutes to stabilize the temperatures. Then he pulled the throttle to off and the engine died.

Removing his helmet, he dried the perspiration off his face with the sleeve of his G-suit as Eddie placed a ladder in position and climbed to the cockpit with the red safety flags for the ejection mechanisms.

"Hi yuh," said Eddie. "You come to see the show, too?"

"Show?" said Judson. "What show?"

He could tell immediately by the odd look Eddie gave him that he'd said the wrong thing.

"The YF-188," said Eddie.

"Oh, sure," said Judson.

"Bixler's had her out on a bunch of taxiing runs," said Eddie. "He said she feels so good he may take her up."

109

"I hope he knows what he's doing," said Judson.

He went down the ladder on awkward, unsteady legs and when he turned away from the airplane and faced the intense sun the heat of the desert lake bed seemed to engulf him all at once, like the breath of a vast cauldron. A sudden whirlwind spun along the row of airplanes, whisking bits of stinging sand into his face.

"God damn," he said, "it's hot."

"Only 105 today," said Eddie. "Practically cool."

"I can see how your teeth are chattering," said Judson. "You going to put the rockets on? I'm supposed to do a target run on a tow sleeve."

"Me and another guy." Eddie glanced at his watch. "She'll be ready in about an hour. We're on call to help on the YF-188."

"Okay," said Judson.

"I heard you had a hairy one in a J the other day," said Eddie.

"Yeah." Judson passed his hand in front of his eyes, wishing the dizziness would go away. "She blew up."

Eddie shook his head. "You were lucky you got out."

"Yeah," said Judson. "Lucky."

He slipped out of his chute, bunched the straps together in one hand to make it an easier load, and walked past the weathered wooden legs of the tall control tower. He placed his flight boots down carefully one after the other on the sandy asphalt, taking pains to walk a straight path, hoping in his wobbly condition that he wouldn't do anything foolish, like falling down or fainting. When he reached the door to the hangar, the exertion of the short walk left him sweating as badly as if he were in the fourth quarter of a varsity football game. But the air-conditioned pilot's lounge was cool and it was like walking into another world, a cool, refreshing world.

He dropped his chute and helmet near one of the chairs and as he straightened up a hand clapped him on the shoulder.

"You're just in time," said Haynes. "Bixler's going to give her another whirl. Come on."

He would have preferred to sit down for a few minutes, but he followed Haynes, White and Spallanzani out the other

110

door of the lounge into the main section of the hangar. A group of men, including a one-star general, two colonels and a major in Air Force blues, were standing with Bixler watching a tractor tow the YF-188 through the open hangar doors. She looked bigger somehow than when Judson had seen her before at the L.A. test hangar. The wings were swept back at a tremendously sharp angle and the top of the wafer-thin rudder was at least two stories above the concrete floor of the hangar. It seemed incredible that such a monster—as big as an airline transport—was designed to carry only one man.

With Judson following a few feet behind, the group of men trailed the YF-188 outside to the strip where the tractor turned her around and a gang of ground crewmen swiftly placed a ladder in position beside the cockpit and connected an external power cart at the rear. Another group of men, including several senior Lansdale engineers, came over from the flight tower and began to chat with Bixler and the general.

Judson was unable to hear what they were talking about. Nor did he particularly care. He was surprised at how pale and tired Bixler looked. There were damp, dark perspiration blotches in the heavy G-suit cloth under Bixler's armpits and the forefinger of his right hand, hanging at his side, was nervously rubbing the callus on the knuckle of his thumb.

He's scared, thought Judson suddenly. *He's as scared as I am.* . . .

The crew chief reported that everything was ready and Bixler walked toward the ladder.

Judson felt abruptly that it was necessary for him to let Bixler know that it was all right, that he didn't mind not doing the test.

He stepped over and offered his hand to Bixler.

"Good luck," he said.

"Thanks," said Bixler. He clasped Judson's hand briefly, his palm moist and cold, but he did not look directly at Judson.

He went up the ladder into the cockpit and Judson moved back and rejoined the other men.

It took Bixler only a comparatively short time to complete his cockpit check-offs. When he achieved ignition, the YF-188's enormous engine became a thundering impossibility with air screaming into the intake duct and shrieking out the tail-

111

pipe and the group of men walked over to the control tower where their eardrums could find some semblance of peace.

Then they turned and watched as Bixler taxied past them toward the strip which led to the runway. Judson felt the ground quiver beneath his feet from the forces of the engine as the airplane went by, bobbing gently on its hydraulics, the hot sun gleaming brightly on the glass-smooth surfaces of the metal wings.

As the YF-188 rolled onto the main runway, the men, with chief engineer Gadford leading the way, went single file up the wooden steps to the glassed-in room at the top of the test control tower. When they were joined by two first lieutenants, the small room became so crowded Garford sent an order to the hangar that no more men were to be admitted. Judson and Spallanzani stood together on the far side of the room, keeping as far away from the brass as possible, looking through the blue-tinted windows and waiting for the airplane to come into view from behind the north hangar about five hundred yards away.

Obdorsk, who was handling the radio and taking notes on a ruled sheet of yellow paper, spoke and the hubbub of voices in the room stilled.

"He's going to try another taxi run," said Obdorsk, switching on the tape recorder.

. In a few moments, the YF-188 came into view and Bixler turned her around until she was facing down the runway.

"This is 978. . . ." Bixler's voice was low and very calm on the loudspeaker. "All clocks normal. . . ."

As Bixler revved her up, the noise of the engine came distinctly into the closed tower room despite the distance that separated the airplane from the tower.With the brakes relased, the YF-188 moved swiftly along, disappearing behind the hangar, reappearing a few seconds later, and gaining speed until it became a small object many thousands of feet away at the far end of the runway.

"Everything satisfactory," radioed Bixler and once more the hubbub of voices in the tower quieted down. "Think I'll try another taxi run, a little faster. . . ."

Obdorsk spoke into the microphone. "How's your tailpipe temp."

"Okay. . . ."

Bixley returned to the starting section of the runway and turned around once more. He revved the engine and there was a new, throatier roar as he cut in the afterburner. Again the airplane rolled along the runway, faster this time, and disappeared behind the hangar.

When he reappeared this time, the airplane was moving very fast.

"Christ!" said the chief engineer, "this is no taxi run—he's going to take her up. . . ."

Chapter Fifteen

JUDSON'S HANDS became hard fists in the pockets of his G-suit and he felt his fingernails cutting into his palms. Trailing a long plume of black smoke, the YF-188 lifted smoothly into the air, the scarlet test boom on the nose aiming upward at a sharp angle.

"My god," breathed Spallanzani beside him. "Beautiful. . . ."

And it was beautiful the way the airplane rose on swift wings, climbing as if with unlimited power, and then banking in a gentle sweep that took it toward the yellow desert hills to the north of the broad dry lake.

All at once the room burst out with the noise of many voices as the tenseness was released. Judson felt himself start to breath again.

"Let me have the mike!" said the chief engineer.

He slipped into Obdorsk's chair and tripped the microphone button.

"Calling 978," Gadford said. "This is North Base Tower calling 978."

"This is 978. . . ." Bixler's voice was distinct despite a flurry of static.

113

"I thought you were going to taxi her," said Gadford.

"Felt good...." said Bixler. "I decided it was time."

"How's your utility system pressure?" said Gadford.

"Right on.... but it's hot in here and getting hotter. I can't get the cockpit cooler to come on...."

"Have you tried the handle on the right console?"

"It won't turn...." Bixler swore. "... stuck."

"Pull it out first and then turn it," said the chief engineer. "You've got to pull it out."

The radio was silent for half a minute and then Bixler came back on.

"Roger and thanks. Working fine, lots of cool air.... I'm going up to 20,000."

"Make this a short one," cautioned Gadford. "No sense doing too much the first time."

"Roger," said Bixler.

The YF-188's wings flashed in the sunlight far to the north and then it sped out of sight.

Judson's pack of cigarettes was damp from where the perspiration had soaked into his shirt pocket. He offered one to Spallanzani.

"God damn," said Spallanzani, "I think I'd rather fly one than watch one. That take-off scared the hell out of me."

But he lighted Judson's cigarette with a match held with firm, steady fingers and Judson was glad it wasn't necessary for him to hold the match because he knew his own fingers would have betrayed him.

There was a crackle of static on the loudspeaker and the men grew silent again as Bixler's voice came in.

"Not going to bother with 20,000.... I'm at 10,000. Tried two half slow rolls and she performed like a doll...."

"What's your position now?" asked Gadford.

"Just passed over Tehachapi.... The go-stick's only at 90 per cent and she's doing 600 knots plus. I'm going to step her up a little...."

"Photo-recorder and oscillograph functioning?" asked Gadford.

"All normal...."

Gadford looked down at the notes he'd penciled on the yellow sheets of paper. He made a minor adjustment on the tape recorder and reached for a cigarette.

114

"He's done enough for one day," Gadford told Obdorsk. "I think we better bring him back."

"Excellent idea, sir," said the general. "No sense overdoing it."

Gadford started to depress the mike button, but Bixler's voice cut in quickly, slurred with excitement, and Judson felt his own heartbeat quicken.

"Jesus, what an airplane!" called Bixler. "Cracked the barrier at Mach 1.35 and didn't even have her wide open...." He paused. "Level flight. Straight-away, level flight...."

The room was quiet for a moment while the significance of Bixler's statement sank in. Then there was an eruption of voices and the general slapped one of the majors on the shoulder and a senior engineer did some quick manipulations with a slide rule.

"That's 991 miles an hour!" announced the senior engineer, his voice hardly carrying over the hubbub. "Fastest a jet's ever gone in straightaway flight!"

"God damn it!" said Spallanzani. He dropped his cigarette on the wooden floor and ground it out with the heel of his flight boot.

Then he looked at Judson. "That ought to be you up there, Jud. That bastard's grabbing your glory!"

Judson shrugged.

"Tower calling 978," said Gadford. "Congratulations!"

The general stepped over to Gadford, spoke into his ear and Gadford depressed the mike button again. "General Eberle also offers his congratulations, Bixler, for a job well done!"

Bixler's voice came in crisply. "Thanks, general...."

"Now get the hell back here," said Gadford, "so we can check that oscillograph and photo recorder."

"Roger," said Bixler. "I'm twenty miles due north and coming in now...."

The men in the tower crowded together in front of the north windows in order to catch the first glimpse of him. In a few moments, a dark speck appeared in the sky. It grew larger and larger still and then the YF-188 streaked silently overhead, its sweptback wings forming a V-shaped silhouette that moved with astonishing speed. The airplane was far, far on the opposite side of the field before its sound—the high, shrill scream of the engine—passed over the tower.

He made a clean, banking turn, came back at about five hundred feet and started a gently-angled approach to the runway.

The angle grew slightly sharper and Judson waited for Bixler to ease her up.

The angle grew sharper.

"Say," said somebody. "Isn't he—"

The tension in the room became so great it was as if the entire space were crisscrossed with fine, taut steel wires. Every eye was on the airplane.

She angled downward, down, down, down toward the yellow, hardpacked floor of the desert and then she began a lazy, uncontrolled roll that put her on her back.

Judson, standing rigidly before the blue-tinted windows, wanted to tear his eyes away, but he could not because he was certain that by some last-second miracle Bixler would pull her out of it.

The airplane hit about a mile away from the tower. One moment it was an airplane and the next moment it was a streak of flame that extended a thousand straight yards along the desert floor and it was no longer an airplane.

A great cloud of black, greasy smoke boiled upward, mixed with yellow dust, and finally Judson was able to pull his eyes away.

The tower was a bedlam of shouts and curses and one of the first lieutenants became violently sick in a wastebasket. Gadford roared into a phone for fire trucks and an ambulance that would not be needed.

Something seemed to go dead inside Judson. He sat down on the chair that had been vacated by the colonel and gripped the edge of one of the desks to steady himself. He stared down at his stiff knuckles which contrasted whitely with the dark mahogany of the desk top and listened to the sounds the other men made as they ran down the wooden tower steps.

When he looked back again, the red flames were no longer visible. A dark smear, smoking blackly, ran for a thousand yards along the desert.

The tower room was deserted except for himself and the miserable first lieutenant. It was silent except for the gentle, whirring sound of the tape recorder's two reels, spinning steadily with nothing to record.

116

Judson reached over and shut off the recorder. Then he got up from the chair, went out the door and walked slowly down the tower steps, keeping his eyes carefully averted so he would not have to look at the spiral of dark smoke.

He went into the hangar and then into the pilot's lounge and began to strip off his damp G-suit, keeping his mind in a tight vacuum, refusing to permit himself to conjecture about what had caused the YF-188 to go in. He got a spare pair of gray slacks out of his locker and put them on and then he hunted through Haynes' and Spallanzani's lockers until he found a half empty bottle of bourbon. He poured a long burning swallow of it down his throat but it failed to relieve the sickness in his stomach and the spidery weaknesses in his legs.

When he left the hangar, walking quickly out into the heat to get away before any of the other men returned, he saw Eddie leaving by another door, carrying a metal toolbox. He didn't want to talk to Eddie, he didn't want to talk to anybody, and he considered ducking back inside the hangar doorway. But Eddie saw him and came over.

Eddie's face was pale.

"God," he said. He mopped the sweat off his face with the back of his hand. "Did you see it?"

Judson nodded.

"He was doing swell," said Eddie. "Leveling off just right and then all of a sudden—"

Eddie wiped his face again and Judson realized there were tears mixed with the sweat and he was surprised because Eddie had never expressed any particular friendliness for Bixler.

"What do you figure happened?" asked Eddie.

"I don't know," said Judson. He turned and started to walk away because he knew if he stayed he might say things he would regret.

"We got the rockets on the J," said Eddie. "She's ready whenever you are."

Judson kept walking, hoping Eddie would think he hadn't heard.

But Eddie caught up, his short legs trying to match strides with Judson's longer ones.

117

"The J's ready," he repeated.

Judson stopped abruptly and as he looked at Eddie he saw from the corner of his eye the thinning tower of black smoke out on the flat desert and he couldn't hold back the damned-up words any longer.

"I'm not going to fly her," he said.

Eddie started to reply but Judson shut him off.

"I've had it," he said, not caring about the tight, angry sounds his voice was making. "I've had it good. I'm not going to fly again—I'm not going to fly the J or a 160K or even a Piper Cub. They can take that $20,000 a year and stick it you-know-where! I don't want any part of it! I don't—"

"Christ's sake, Jud!" said Eddie, "you don't have to tell me. I—"

"Label me what you want!" said Judson. "Call me a yellow-bellied coward, I don't care! I've had it, that's all!"

He stood there, staring at Eddie, waiting for Eddie to say something, feeling the hot, sticky sweat inside his shirt and wishing he were a thousand, thousand miles away, back at Hamburg or Marseille—where he'd never lacked confidence—or even back at Seoul where everything had turned out all right even on the bad days.

"I don't blame you," said Eddie, quietly. "Lord, I don't blame you a bit, Jud."

"Thanks," said Judson.

He left Eddie and walked along the drab-yellow flank of the hangar, shielding his eyes from the hot gusts of wind. At the security gate, the guard said something to him and Judson mumbled an acknowledgement although he did not know and didn't care what the guard had said. Across the asphalt road from the hangar, there was a waiting bench for the bus. He sat on it for a long time until he saw Haynes and Spallanzani come out to the parking area. He didn't want to talk to them nor did he want the lift that he knew they would offer so he got up from the bench and stood behind the large wooden sign that said *Warning—Restricted Area* and waited there until they drove away in Haynes' dust-covered Porche.

A blue Air Force bus came along finally and took him from the north base across the sandy wastes to the area of weathered quonset huts that was the administration center. He caught another bus there which took him to Lancaster where he caught a

Greyhound for Los Angeles. And all during the slow, noisy ride he kept thinking about Bixler's three kids, the wife Bixler was separated from and the other women he'd been running around with and the fact that like the rest of them he didn't have any life insurance. The messes that people made of their lives—how did they start? And where was the turning-back point? He knew he had to see Chally right away and tell her he'd quit flying. Because maybe that was it. Maybe that was the real reason she wouldn't live with him—because she feared that some day she might get the same message that Mrs. Bixler would get this afternoon and she wanted to get away, get out of his life before it happened.

That had to be the reason. There was no other reason that made sense.

Chapter Sixteen

AT THE DOWNTOWN BUS DEPOT, he boarded a cab and drove to Chally's newest apartment in Hollywood. It was about five in the afternoon when he got there and he'd made up his mind to tell her everything, even the fact that he'd spent the night with Marjorie. They would have to start off entirely new with everything that had happened before permanently behind them.

He cursed when his urgent pressure on the door-bell brought no reaction. Going back down the stairs, he hunted up the building superintendent and received the information that although Chally hadn't been seen around the place since the preceding morning she hadn't moved out since her things were still in the apartment.

For an hour and a half, he waited in the lobby. When she did not appear, he hailed another cab and, frustrated and angry, leaned back against the rear seat cushion and closed his eyes. It was too late in the evening to call MGM and see if she were rehearsing. There was no telling where else she might be—out with friends, at the theater or a party.

"Well, to hell with her!" he said, thinking aloud.

The cab driver's head twisted around. "D'you say something, fella?"

"Nothing important," said Judson.

He got out of the cab at the plant and drove home in the Jaguar. When he came in the back door, Opal was finishing washing the dinner dishes but, as she did whenever he was late, she had kept a plateful of food warming in the oven.

"You go wash up," she told him. "It'll be ready when you get back."

Nodding, he went into the bathroom. Before he turned the water on in the bowl he was joined by his father. His father's face, reflected over his shoulder in the mirror, was drawn and grim.

"I heard about what happened to Bixler...." His father's voice was strained. "It's been on the radio all day."

Judson kept on lathering his hands.

"I want you to know I'm sorry," said his father.

Judson rinsed the lather off.

"And it's driving me crazy!" his father burst out. "The strain we're all under, never knowing whether you'll be the next one. Never knowing when—"

"I quit today," said Judson.

There was a moment of silence.

"You what?" said his father.

"I'm not going to fly any more." Judson finished drying his face with the blue towel and draped it carefully over its chrome rack.

His father seized his arm and turned him around until they were face to face.

"Are you telling me the truth?"

Judson nodded wearily. "God damn it, Dad, I'm no little kid any more. I told you I've quit flying and that's it—I've quit."

"Thank god!" said his father, but there was still doubt and disbelief on his features.

Judson ran a comb through his dark hair and then left the bathroom and walked out to the kitchen. His father followed.

"Does this mean you'll take that job I offered?" asked his father. "I'll make you vice president in charge of engineering on that new canning machinery."

"I guess so," said Judson. "But not right away. I've got to have time to think and see if I'm doing the right thing."

"Of course, son, of course. You realize I'll only be able to pay you $8000 to start, not nearly what Lansdale pays you. But there'll be more later and I know you won't regret your decision once you start putting that mind of yours to work. All it takes is—"

"Let's not talk about it," said Judson. "Except there's one thing I want you to understand. I don't care about the money one way or the other. The $20,000 Lansdale's been paying was swell, nice to have, but that wasn't why I flew. I flew because I liked it." He sat down at the table and rubbed his hand across his eyes. "And now I don't like to fly any more. It's as simple as that."

"All right," said his father, "we won't talk about it any more for now. You take it easy for a few days. When you feel like coming around to the factory, come around. Your office will be waiting."

Judson nodded and as his father left the room he began to eat the food Opal set before him. The roast beef tasted dry and leathery and the green peas were shrunken and dented from their wait in the oven. He forced himself to eat mouthful after mouthful and then gradually he became aware that Dunc had been standing in the doorway for some time watching him.

"Hello, pipe jockey," said Judson.

"Hi." Dunc put his small hands in the pockets of his faded jeans.

Washing the meat and potatoes down with coffee, Judson managed to swallow several more mouthfuls.

"I heard what you were saying to Dad," said Dunc. "Are you really going to quit?"

"Yes," said Judson.

"Is it because of what happened to Bixler?"

"Partly."

Glistening, almost on the verge of tears, Dunc's blue eyes were large and upset. "You're never going to fly again—not ever?"

Judson shrugged, wishing he could change the subject. "We can always fly your models. That's flying, isn't it?"

But Dunc wasn't to be led aside that easily.

"Are you afraid to fly?" he said. "Is that it?"

Judson couldn't face the intense blue eyes any longer. Rising from the table with his dishes, he began to rinse them in the sink.

"I never thought you'd be afraid. . . . " Dunc's voice broke. "I never thought—"

Judson stacked the plates. When he turned away from the sink, Dunc was walking, almost running, through the dining room. And then up the stairs.

Judson followed and he arrived at the doorway of Dunc's room just in time to see Dunc cross to the work table on which his model parts were spread out, pick up the green-tissue covered fuselage of his airplane and smash it down against the wing again and again until there was nothing left but a scattering of broken balsa sticks to which clung tattered bits of paper.

Then Dunc threw himself on his bed and began to cry. It was muffled crying, deep in his throat, the crying of a boy who was trying to keep from acting like a boy but failing.

Remaining in the doorway, Judson waited until the sobbing slackened before going over and sitting at the foot of the bed.

"I'm sorry, Dunc," he said, "I'm sorry about the whole lousy mess. But why take it out on your airplane—after all the hours of work you put in on it?"

Dunc buried his face deeper into his pillow. "If you're through with flying, I'm through with flying. To hell with it!"

"Okay, partner," said Judson softly. "To hell with it."

"I'm going to swear plenty from now on," said Dunc. "To hell with everything. To hell with the airplane. To hell with Dad. To hell with you, too, Jud!"

"All right, all right," cautioned Judson. "No need to over do it."

He went over to the dresser, took a clean handkerchief from the top drawer and put it in Dunc's hand.

"Okay," he said, "dry 'em off."

Dunc ignored the handkerchief.

"You broke your promise," he said, "and I never thought you'd do a thing like that."

122

"What promise?" asked Judson although he knew well enough what Dunc meant.

"You promised to let me see you fly a test. . . ." Dunc's shoulders quivered as he tried manfully to keep from breaking into tears again. "Now I'll never get to see one. Never!"

"I wouldn't say that," said Judson. "I can always take you over to watch one of the other fellows fly one."

"No!" Dunc sat up, his face red and creased where he had pressed it against the pillow. "That wouldn't be the same. I want to see *you* fly one!"

The blue eyes looked at Judson for a long accusing moment during which he tried desperately to think of a reply that might win him back some small measure of respect. But he failed. It was as though his brain had been squeezed dry of its ability to think. He got up from the bed, looked down at Dunc and then went over to the work table. He picked up one of the splintered balsa sticks, turned it over in his fingers and put it back on the table. Then he went to his own room.

He tried to read but it was no good. His mind refused to concentrate on the words and his hands fidgeted with the magazine pages. Turning on the radio was no improvement— the music was inane and tuneless and the dramatic shows were transparent and contrived. He knew there was a bottle of White Horse under the shirts in his bureau drawer—a nice new bottle, unopened—but he forced himself to resist it. Once he found himself walking toward the closet, ready to get his coat and go to Ditman's. But he knew that would be a mistake—he couldn't possibly face Spallanzani and Haynes after the way he'd walked off the field at Edwards.

He went into the bathroom, took a shower and put on his pajamas. Then he turned out the lights and went to bed. Sleep was a long time coming but he made it finally and it was all right until somewhere deep in the devious channels of his brain a nightmare began to grow. He saw the YF-188 going in, turning on its back and going in, going in, and he tried to warn Bixler. He shouted at Bixler, screamed at him to eject, to get out before it was too late. But it was already too late and there was flame and smoke and the pounding of feet on the tower steps and he jerked upright in bed so quickly that he got a cramp in the calf of his left leg. Massaging the

123

muscle, he stared into the darkness of the room, remembering how it had been, remembering every detail down to how the sunlight had flashed on the YF-188's stabilizer just before the second of impact.

Very quickly he got out of bed and limped over to the bureau. With cold sweaty fingers that were inept in the darkness, he got out the bottle of White Horse, removed the stamp and the cork and tilted it up for a long swallow. He got back into bed, still holding the bottle, and kept drinking until the blessed moment arrived when in a haze of relaxation he lowered the bottle to the floor with a limp arm and went back to sleep.

In the morning he was awakened by Opal's knuckles rapping on the door.

"Jud," she called. "Wake up. Telephone."

"Yeah," he mumbled.

The hands of the electric clock on the bureau were angled at 9:15. He got out of bed slowly, walked on bare feet into his father's bedroom and picked up the extension phone.

"Hello," he said.

"Good morning, Mr. Judson," replied a crisp, feminine voice. "This is Mr. Lansdale's secretary. He would like to see you in his office as soon as possible. Will 10 o'clock be all right?"

"Yes," said Judson, "but—"

"Very good," she said. "he'll see you at 10."

She hung up.

Judson put the phone back on its ebony cradle. There was a dull ache just behind his forehead from the whiskey and his mouth was dry. He hadn't expected it to come this quickly. Usually it took longer for reports, like on the 160K's smashed oleo strut and the J blow-up, to reach the old man. He wished he'd put in his resignation the day before and thus avoided the unpleasant scene that was coming up.

After a quick shave, he put on a fresh white shirt, a copper-colored tie with embroidered Hawaiian figures and his new gray flannel suit. He ate some toast, drank a cup of coffee and drove straight to the plant, arriving in the waiting room adjacent to Lansdale's office at five minutes to ten.

A half hour passed before the secretary told him to go in.

It was an enormous office of paneled oak with a picture

124

window that permitted a clear view of the plant and the runways. As Judson entered, Lansdale was seated at his desk, chin propped in his hands, features engrossed in thought, but he got up when he saw Judson.

"Morning, Jud," he said. "Glad you could make it."

He was a big man, in his early fifties, as tall as Judson, with a sunburned complexion and as they shook hands Judson noticed again the thin white V-shaped scar on Lansdale's chin, a scar he'd received in a crash during a Thompson Trophy race in the days before he'd become a successful manufacturer.

"I came back from Washington last night," said Lansdale. "Left as soon as I heard what happened to Bixler."

"It was a bad one," said Judson.

"Yes," said Lansdale. He clenched his teeth and a knot of muscle alternately appeared and disappeared in the area of his chin near the white scar. "Even though he didn't complete the tests, I've made arrangements for the bonus to be paid to Mrs. Bixler. But, of course, that isn't why I wanted to talk to you, Jud."

He indicated a leather armchair across from his desk. "You might as well be comfortable—I've got quite a few things to say."

Here it comes, thought Judson. He knew Lansdale would let him down gently. It wasn't Lansdale's nature to be rough and tough in these matters but after it was all over he would be just as thoroughly fired as if it had happened the moment he stepped in the door.

"All of us," said Lansdale, "the engineers, the designers and myself are mystified. We can't figure out why the YF-188 went in. You got any ideas, Jud?"

Judson shook his head. "He seemed to have perfect control, and then all of a sudden he went over on his back as if he didn't have any control at all. . . ."

From a polished walnut box on the desk Lansdale took a cigarette. He offered one to Judson and lit it with a large silver table lighter. For a minute they smoked in silence, with Lansdale staring thoughtfully at a scale model of the YF-188 which stood on the desk and Judson wishing that he'd hurry up, fire him and get it over with.

"I can't understand it," said Lansdale. "It was a spectacular flight, broke every jet speed record in the book and then—"

125

His voice dropped to a lower, more confidential tone. "I'll tell you something, Jud, something that's supposed to be a secret. We've got millions tied up in the YF-188. And we've got to find out whether the airplane was at fault or whether it was a pilot error."

"How are you going to find out?" said Judson. "Weren't the photo panel and oscillograph records smashed all to hell?"

"Yes," said Lansdale, "but there's another way."

He spun the heavy, stainless steel combination knob on the vault in the wall beside his desk. Swinging the door back, he went inside and then returned carrying a thick roll of blue-prints.

"I want you to see these, Jud," he said.

He spread the blue prints open on the desk and motioned for Judson to come around behind it. His first glimpse of the specifications told Judson that here was an airplane to out-perform all airplanes. Its designation was X-14A. It had a long, slim fuselage, so lengthy it made the swept-back wing seem stubby by comparison. A cutaway scale drawing ex-plained the need for all that fuselage. The airplane would be rocket-powered and an extraordinary amount of fuselage space would be taken up by the fuel tanks. Quickly, Judson's eyes skimmed some of the other details—the cockpit silhouette that provided a minimum amount of wind resistance, the para-chute brake at the tail and the razor-thin airfoils.

"You're an engineer," said Lansdale, "so I don't have to tell you that the X-14A is purely an experimental aircraft for research. We figure that if she's ever flown all-out she'll do over 2000 miles an hour."

"Christ," said Judson.

"I don't blame you for being impressed," said Lansdale. "I'm just as impressed as you are. She'll use lox, liquid oxygen, for fuel, of course, and we'll drop her from the belly of a B-29."

Judson nodded. "When are you going to start work on her?"

"Start?" Lansdale laughed and took another cigarette from the polished walnut box. "The X-14A has been the most care-fully-guarded secret since the atom bomb. It's already been built. It was assembled at our Ohio plant, with final finishing at Edwards."

Judson shook his head in amazement and looked at Lansdale intently to see if he were serious.

"It's true," said Lansdale. "The X-14A has been at Edwards for weeks."

"I've never heard even one rumor about it," said Judson. "All we've ever heard was talk about the YF-188."

"Actually there's a similarity," said Lansdale.

He selected one of the blueprints, carefully rolled it flat and his tobacco-stained forefinger pointed out details of the wing.

"You'll notice, Jud," he said, "that the X-14A's wing is practically the same as the YF-188's. And that's why we built the X-14A in the first place. We've sunk the whole future of the corporation into that wing. Engineers in Washington have told me I'm crazy to attempt to fly a sweptback wing in the higher supersonic ranges. And I had a hell of a fight with some of my own designers over it, too."

Lansdale turned and looked out the broad window as an F-160K rolled down the runway and they both watched it lift into the air and bank swiftly away. Then Lansdale sat down in his leather armchair and pushed his fingers through his thick, iron-gray hair. Quite suddenly his ruddy face looked drawn and tired.

"Here it is in a nutshell, Jud." He spoke slowly, his words weighted with deliberation. "We figured the YF-188 wing, with only a few changes, would be good at all speeds, jet-powered in the YF-188, rocket-powered in the X-14A. Now, because of Bixler's crash, we don't know. And the Air Force, General Eberle especially, told me last night that we've either got to start production right away on the YF-188 or junk it. So we've got to find out— and the X-14A is going to be the test. If we can fly that wing at Mach 2 or faster, maneuver it and then land it, we'll know the YF-188 design is all right and that something else caused Bixler's crash."

Judson picked up the blueprint and re-examined the remarkably thin construction of the wing. He looked at Lansdale.

"So it's as simple as that," he said. "If the X-14A's a success then the YF-188 will be a success and you can start production and start getting back your millions."

"Right," said Lansdale.

They both fell silent and watched another F-160K pause at the head of the runway and prepare to take off.

"You see, Jud," said Lansdale after a moment. "It's all up to you."

"Up to me?" Judson turned slowly and looked at Lansdale. "Why me?"

"Who else do you think is going to fly the X-14A?" said Lansdale.

·

Chapter Seventeen

JUDSON TRIED not to let his face show how he felt inside. He did not reply immediately but remained seated on the edge of the desk looking out over the airfield.

"Naturally with Bixler gone you're taking over as senior test pilot," said Lansdale.

Afraid to trust himself to speak, Judson merely nodded.

"And I want you to spend the rest of the day familiarizing yourself with the X-14A's details," said Lansdale. "We've simplified the instrument panel and consoles as much as possible so there won't be as much to learn as you might think. We've got the initial take-off scheduled for tomorrow morning at seven, but we can delay it a day if you need more time."

"Tomorrow?" said Judson.

"There's no need horsing around with delays," said Lansdale. "The X-14A is as ready as she's ever going to be and there's—"

He was interrupted by the inter-com buzzer on his desk. Flicking the switch, he told his secretary to wait a moment and then glanced back at Judson.

"There's an awful lot of pressure from the Air Force," he continued, "to get the test done right away. They're so all-fired anxious they want an Air Force major to fly the X-14A but I talked them out of that because I feel there's only one man qualified for the job, Jud, and that man's you."

As Lansdale turned his attention back to the inter-com, a rush of thoughts went through Judson's mind, with each individual thought clamoring for individual attention. It was incredible. He'd come here expecting to be fired....and here he was being assigned the most important job of all ... senor test pilot ... for an airplane capable of going 2000 miles an hour ... rocket power ... seven o'clock the next morning....

"All right, all right," said Lansdale into the inter-com. "You can send him in."

He looked at Judson and shrugged. "General Eberle's outside waiting to see me with ants in his pants about something. Here—" He picked the scattered blueprints up from his desk and handed them to Judson. "Take these into my other office and start studying them."

He opened a gleaming paneled oak door and showed Judson inside the other office.

"Listen," said Judson, "there's something I've got to tell you. Like the other day in the J, for example and—"

"Later," said Lansdale curtly. "I'll talk to you later." He went out, closing the door behind himself and grumbling. "Generals. God damn generals."

The room, with its thick carpeting and soundproof walls, became very silent.

Judson sat down on a dark blue leather divan and unrolled one of the blueprints. His eyes scanned the drawings and read the specifications but the information didn't get through to his brain because his mind was still off on a whirl of its own, trying to rationalize the enormity of what was happening. It was obvious that all the men—Spallanzani, Haynes, White and Eddie—had protected him, covered for him, and word of his walk-out the day before at Edwards had not gotten back to Lansdale. And it was possible, too, that Bixler had protected him by not reporting his pilot's error aboard the J. Which meant that in the eyes of Lansdale he was still the pilot he had always been, qualified to fly the X-14A.

But I'm not qualified. The voice was like a record in his mind, a spinning record playing over and over again. *I'm not qualified. I don't want to fly the X-14A. I'm afraid.*

He got up from the divan and walked to the door, suddenly feeling fortified enough to go out and tell Lansdale he couldn't do it. But before his hand touched the brass doorknob, the door swung back and Lansdale strode in. He was all business and in a hurry.

"Jud," he said. "I'm going over to the Federal Building with General Eberle. Got to meet some other brass." He went to the desk and signed a card which he handed to Judson. "Here's a special pass. I'll let you into that restricted Building L2 at Edwards. I want you to go there this afternoon and sit in the cockpit of the X-14A and get everything checked out. Okay?"

"Listen," said Judson, "there's something I've got to tell you."

"Can't it wait?" said Lansdale.

"No, damn it," said Judson. "I want you to know about what happened in the J that blew up the other day. It was caused by pilot error—*my* error. And then there's—"

"So what?" said Lansdale. "Everybody makes a mistake once in a while. Just make sure you don't make one tomorrow, that's all."

Lansdale strode out, slamming the door behind him, and once more the room became silent.

Judson went back to the divan. For a long time he sat there, smoking cigarette after cigarette, trying to think of a way out, a reasonable way out, but he could see none. He picked up the blueprints and began studying them in detail, noting that the X-14A's skin was stainless steel with tough titanium at the important contact points to resist melting from prolonged friction with the air at ultra supersonic speeds. A cutaway showed how the entire cockpit section could be jettisoned in an emergency. Other specifications showed that the tanks in the elongated fuselage held three tons of rocket fuel to be fired in four stages and there was room enough in the nose for half a ton of research instruments.

He remained in the office for two hours, pouring over the specifications until his brain was swimming in formulae, sines and cosines. Then he turned the blueprints over to one of Lansdale's vice presidents and left the administration building. A yellow company bus took him over to the hangar section and he arrived just as one of the shuttle Navions was warming up for its run to the desert.

Forty-five minutes later, the Navion taxied up to the flight operations center at Edwards and Judson got out. It was hotter than it had been the previous day and the heat, whipped off the floor of the desert by the wind, beat at him furiously as he walked over to Building L2.

The building was not particularly large. There was the usual high barbed wire fence around it and he realized he had seen the building many times before but had not considered it significant. Two uniformed Air Police stood at the gate and they scrutinized Judson's pass for a lengthy two minutes and made notes in three different record books before admitting him.

The interior of the building was dimly-lighted and almost silent except for the quiet conversation of several electronics men doing some wiring at a work bench.

His heels echoing hollowly in the rafters, Judson walked across the concrete floor to the X-14A.

He halted and stared at it and his throat went dry.

No real implication of the size of the airplane had been contained in the blueprints. It was gigantic—far, far larger than the YF-188 and far deadlier looking. It hugged the concrete low on its three wheels and its slim fuselage from the tail to the needle-pointed test boom on the nose looked as long as a Constellation. Reflecting the light from the naked bulbs overhead, its stainless steel surfaces gleamed as if polished by hand with jeweler's rouge. Not a rivet head, not a welding joint or an unnecessary crack or crevice interrupted the smoothness of the swept-back wing. In proportion to the long fuselage, the thin tapering wing looked small and it seemed impossible that it could generate enough lift to keep the giant in the air.

He walked to the tail and looked into the openings of the rocket barrels. Then he went around to the ladder and started up to the cockpit.

While he was looking through the windshield, getting his first glimpse of the maze of unfamiliar instruments, the clanks hit.

Without warning, his muscles quivered and the nausea washed through him in deepening waves. Everything went gray and then black and he fell against the ladder, cheek pressing against the cool metal of one of the rungs, hands holding on like desperate claws. He tried to vomit but the cramps in his stomach would not let him.

He didn't know how long he clung there, afraid any mo-

131

ment one of the electronics' men would discover him. When some semblance of strength returned to his legs, he lowered himself slowly rung by rung to the concrete floor. He sat on a packing case and he knew there was no sense trying to kid himself. He got them now merely by being close to an airplane. What if he got them while he was up in the X-14A? It would be foolhardy to run the risk. If Lansdale wanted the god damn airplane flown tomorrow, let the Air Force fly it. Let their eager-beaver major fly it. And the sooner he told Lansdale the better.

On unsteady legs, he walked to the phone booth near a group of lathes and drill presses at the far corner of the building. He got the proper number of coins into the slot, but only after he dropped a quarter on the floor and spent half a minute looking for it while the operator's voice repeated: "Seventy cents for three minutes, sir. Seventy cents for—"

"All right!" he bellowed. "All right!"

He got the Los Angeles office finally and asked for Lansdale. Instead, Lansdale's secretary came on.

"I'm sorry, Mr. Judson," she said, "but Mr. Lansdale's still in conference at the Federal Building. Is there any message?"

"No, god damn it!" said Judson, "there's no message!"

Hanging up, he knew he had acted like a petty, frustrated child, but he didn't care. He didn't care about anything any more except Chally. And the chance to live a normal life with her like any normal man and wife, free from everlasting fear and worry, free from tensions that tore the guts out of a man.

He went back to the flight operations center and boarded another Navion. All during the flight to Los Angeles he sat uncomfortably on the rear seat, admiring the easy, competent way the young pilot handled the light airplane. As soon as the wheels stopped rolling on the L.A. taxiing strip, he got out and went into a phone booth in the test hangar.

Again Lansdale's secretary answered. Her tone was cool.

"Sorry, Mr. Judson, but Mr. Lansdale is attending a cocktail party for the Undersecretary of the Air Force."

"When will he be through?"

"He didn't say, but I know he'll be attending a reception afterward at the Statler. I told him you called and he said to tell you it's been confirmed that the take-off will be tomorrow at seven. Do you have any message for him?"

"Yes," said Judson. "Tell him I want to see him."

"Will tomorrow be all right?"

"No!" Judson felt the anger rising again. "Tomorrow will *not* be all right. I want to see him tonight and it can't wait!"

"If he calls I'll tell him," she said. "Will that be all, Mr. Judson? I've got another phone ringing."

"That's all," said Judson.

He hung up, cursing the cold, impersonal serenity of secretaries, cursing his headache, cursing his clumsy fingers when he broke a cigarette getting it out of the pack. He dialed 113 for information and asked if there was a phone listed for Chally at her new address. There was and he dialed the number. The phone rang and rang but there was no answer. On the hunch that he might have dialed the wrong number, he dialed it once more and again it rang and rang, the metallic ringing sound in the receiver mocking his anxiety and disappointment until he hung up.

He was walking away from the phone booth when it occurred to him that Chally's friend Lisa might be persuaded to tell where Chally could be reached. Returning to the booth, he phoned plant personnel just before the office closed for the night and got Lisa's home address. Again he dialed 113 but there was no phone listed for Lisa and he decided it might be worth while to go out to Lisa's place and talk to her about Chally. He recalled the obscure, detached expression in Lisa's eyes at their last meeting and how he'd been almost certain she'd been concealing information about Chally. He decided to be tough with her. Maybe that was the way to chip her veneer.

It was nearly six o'clock when he parked the Jaguar in front of the gray stucco duplex with the red shutters that the office had listed as Lisa's address. There was a neat lawn in front bounded by a low yellow-green boxwood hedge. A double row of rose trees framed the concrete walk to the small porch.

He pressed the doorbell button and the musical sound of chimes came through the open front door from somewhere in the back of the house. Through the screen door, he saw a lamp burning on an end table and scattered newspapers on the rug. He rang the chimes again and as his eyes became more accustomed to the interior light, he saw cocktail glasses on the maple arm of a divan and a coffee table on which there was a tray of sandwiches.

After a reasonable wait, he pressed the doorbell button again and still there was no answer, nor was there any sound of footsteps in the house although the cocktail glasses, the lighted lamp and the sandwiches indicated someone was home. He stood closer to the screen door and obtained a better view of the interior. He saw a magenta-walled hallway and a small slice of bedroom. The bedroom was dim but there was enough light for him to see a foot extending past the edge of a bed.

It was a small foot, obviously feminine because of the fluffy, pom-pom-decorated mule which hung by a loose strap from the toes.

He pressed the button several times in quick succession until the house was filled with repeating music of the chimes but the foot did not move.

"Hello," he said through the screen door. "Anybody home in there?"

There was no reply and the foot did not move.

Chapter Eighteen

HE TESTED the screen door and found it was unlatched. Opening it, he stepped into the living room and let the door slam noisily behind him.

"Hello?" he said. "Are you awake in there, Lisa?"

The silence continued. As he walked across the living room, he noticed that the sandwiches on the coffee table were curled and dry-looking. He went down the short hall and stepped into the bedroom.

The light from the living room was not enough to illuminate the bedroom. His fingers found the wall switch and he flipped

134

it and then he saw that the foot was Lisa's and she was lying on her back on the bed asleep.

He started to speak again and then he realized that there was something not right about her.

She was too silent, too absolutely unmoving to be asleep. He went toward her around the foot of the bed and then for the first time he noticed the other single bed and the other girl on it, resting on her side with her back to him.

It took him an instant to realize from the short dark hair and the graceful slope of the shoulder that it was Chally.

For a moment, he was too startled to speak.

Then he said: "Chally?"

He spoke again, louder. "Chally!"

She did not stir.

Approaching her, he reached out to waken her. Her shoulder was cold, as cold as stainless steel, and as soon as he touched it he knew what was the matter, knew why she hadn't heard him, knew with horror why she lay so silently.

"Chally!" His voice was a cry deep in his throat.

He threw himself on the bed beside her and afraid to, not wanting to, he found her wrist and put his fingers against the cold soft flesh. There was no movement, no pulse beat.

He could not believe it. He saw her lying there, eyes closed, long beautiful lashes casting shadows on her cheeks, lips softly together and he could not believe she was dead.

It was as though he were in a trance. Slowly he moved from her side and turned to the other bed. His fingers went automatically to Lisa's wrist and it was the same. No pulse beat. He was not surprised. Nor did he think that anything anywhere could ever surprise him again. He was beyond surprising.

His eyes went numbly around the room, saw the litter of whiskey glasses, the magazines and scattered clothing on the floor—and saw the two empty bottles that had contained sleeping pills.

He stepped over to the dressing table and forced himself to read the two notes which lay among the jars of skin creams and colognes. One was written by Lisa, the other by Chally.

Very slowly he read Chally's words, some scratched out, hastily written in ink on the same peach-colored stationery she had used for the very first letter she had written him.

"Dearest Jud:

"I know the terrible thoughts you will have of me after you read this and you will be right because I am awful, an awful person. Something is wrong with me—something deep and awful inside and now I want to be honest with you for the first time. I had a terrible love affair in high school. Not with a boy. A girl. It has always been that way with me and I thought if I married someone I admired, someone strong and masculine like you that it would help me. But it didn't work. Lord knows I tried, Jud, tried so hard. And I do love you—in my own way I love you. But I'm rotten. I could not stay away from Lisa. I hate her, oh, how I hate her, hate her, but I cannot stay away from her! I am guilty. Lisa is guilty. And, God give us strength, we are going to try to take the only way out of this hopeless, hopeless mess. Please try to forget you ever knew me, Jud."

The note was signed with a simple initial "C."

He read it through again, sick inside and growing sicker, and dropped it on the top of the dressing table.

Turning, he looked at her again, at the calm, childlike expression on her face and the beautiful line of her throat. It was impossible. Incredibly, fantastically impossible.

He did not know how long he remained with them in the room. After an interval he found himself looking for the telephone. Failing to find it, he went out the front door and walked along the sidewalk to the house next door. He hardly saw the man who answered his ring and he did not know what he said to him but the man let him in and showed him to the telephone. He said what he had to say to the police and then he returned to the duplex and sat on the divan, looking at the dried-up sandwiches on the coffee table but not really seeing them.

They came after a while, uniformed men and some not in uniform. He remained on the divan while they talked to him in quiet, efficient tones and wrote in their notebooks. He didn't know how long the questioning continued. One of the men brought him a tumbler containing two inches of whiskey and he drank it quickly, scarcely tasting it.

They asked questions and more questions.

136

Once he heard a voice in the bedroom, a voice that was somewhat louder than the others and which spoke with authority. ". . . dead since about 5 a.m., this morning, I'd judge," the voice said. "Probably took the dose last night. . . ."

Finally they were through with him and told him he could leave.

He walked outside and sat down in the Jaguar. After a while he started the engine and pulled away from the curb. He found it very hard to decide where to go.

Chapter Nineteen

HE DID NOT WANT to go to Ditman's. He could not face the lights and the laughter. Nor could he go home to his father and Dunc—he wasn't ready to talk to them about it.

He drove without thinking, stopping for traffic signals, shifting gears, treading the brake pedal automatically until on an unfamiliar street somewhere he decided that the person he wanted to see, the person he wanted to talk to, was Marjorie.

He drove slowly but he took the most direct route, parking in her driveway. When she came to the door, he could tell by the way she looked at him that she knew something was wrong.

"Jud!" she said. She drew the door further back so he could enter. "What's happened?"

"I've got to have time to think," he muttered. "Time to figure out what I've got to do. . . ."

For a few minutes she said nothing more. While he sat stiffly on the divan, she was busy in the kitchen and he heard the tinkle of ice cubes in glasses as she returned carrying a tray.

"This will help," she said, handing him a bourbon and water. "Have you had anything to eat?"

He shook his head and took a long swallow of the liquor.

"I've never seen you look so pale," she said. "Do you want to tell me about it?"

137

He took another swallow and felt it finally down in his chest and warm in his belly.

"Chally's dead," he said, the words strangely matter-of-fact and impersonal. "And Lisa's dead."

Then while she listened in stunned silence, her eyes never leaving his face, he told her about it, all about it, leaving out none of the details.

When he finished, covering his face with his hands in an effort to blot out the picture of them lying so quietly on the two single beds, Marjorie came over to him. She laid her hand gently on his shoulder.

"I'm sorry, Jud," she said, "so terribly sorry. I never dreamed it could end like that—" She paused. "Or perhaps I would have told you. Perhaps I should have told you anyway."

He glanced up at her. "Told me what?"

"I worked in the same office with them for a while," she said. "In little ways, in little things that they did, I could see the attraction they had for one another."

"For christ's sake!" He looked at her harshly. "Why didn't you tell me?"

Marjorie did not reply immediately. When she spoke her voice was low. "Would you have believed me, Jud?"

He hesitated.

"No," he said. "I guess not. . . . I can't even believe it now."

For a time they were silent. Judson finished his bourbon and water and Marjorie went out to the kitchen, mixed him another and brought it to him. He drank half of it and then got up from his chair.

"I've got to phone Lansdale," he said. "I've got to tell him I'm not going to do it."

"Do what?"

"Fly the X-14A in the morning."

"The X-14A?" Her eyes looked at him with surprise.

"It's restricted but I guess I can tell you," he said. "It's an experimental job. Very supersonic. And if Lansdale thinks I'm going to fly it, he's crazy. He can get another boy."

He walked into the bedroom, picked up the phone and began to dial.

Marjorie came in.

"Jud," she said, "are you sure that's what you want to do? You've never turned down a test job before."

"You don't know the half of it." Judson laughed—a short, bitter laugh. "I turned down a job yesterday, walked right off the field without doing it. My nerves are shot. . . ."

He held up his hand, displaying his trembling fingers.

"Look at them," he said, "look at them shake. And what do you expect after what I saw tonight, after the way I saw her lying there? In the shape I'm in I can't be trusted to fly even a—" He groped for the right word, failed to find it and finished lamely—"A Piper Cub."

He didn't like the way Marjorie looked at him as he compelled dialing Lansdale's home number. It wasn't a lack of respect; it was something else.

Lansdale's maid answered the phone and said Lansdale was still at the reception at the Statler.

Judson hung up and turned the pages of the phone book, hunting for the hotel's number.

Marjorie stepped closed to him.

"Jud," she said quietly. "I don't think you should phone him. Or at least think it over."

"Why?" he said, wishing she wouldn't interfere.

"Because I think you should fly it, Jud. And I hope you won't think I'm saying this because I want to."

"Are you crazy?" he said. "Do you have any idea how much this test means to the plant? It means everything. That god damn airplane is capable of 2000 miles an hour and If I smash it to smithereens then you and every other Lansdale worker will be fresh out of a job the day after tomorrow. What if I get the clanks while I'm up there?"

The expression in her dark blue eyes changed, not a great deal but enough to tell him his point had gone home.

"The clanks?" she said. "You've had them?"

"Every god damn day this week. And I've had it. That's all there is to it—I've had it."

He found the Statler's number and dialed it angrily while Marjorie watched him in silence. Finally, after talking to several minor hotel officials, he was told that Lansdale was making a speech at the reception and could not be interrupted.

Judson returned to the living room and sat down. He finished the rest of the bourbon in his glass while Marjorie attended to details in the kitchen. When she came back, she carried a tray on which were some deviled ham sandwiches and sliced yellow sponge cake.

"Thanks," he said, taking one of the sandwiches.

But when he bit into it he remembered the dry, curled sandwiches on the coffee table in Lisa's house and suddenly the bread in his mouth tasted dry and he found it hard to swallow. He put the sandwich back on the tray.

"Would you like something else?" said Marjorie. "There's some potato salad in the refrigerator."

He shook his head.

For what seemed like a long time, they did not speak. Marjorie sat in the brown frieze armchair across from him, holding a piece of cake but not eating it, and then their eyes met.

"I want to tell you something, Jud," she said. "After George was killed my Mother and Dad wanted me to go back to Seattle to live. Well, I went back there and stayed for a few months but it was all wrong. I kept thinking about George and the work he'd been doing which had meant so much to him. I'd never had a job in the airplane business before but I decided that I should—that I should work at Lansdale so I might find out what it was that meant so much to George."

"Did you find out?" Judson said.

"Yes, I did."

Marjorie placed the cake, still untouched, back on the tray.

"I found out that you pilots don't fly just for the thrill of it —not any more, not when you're in your thirties. Nor do you fly for the money because any fool knows there isn't enough money in the whole world to pay for the chances you take. So I think you test these planes, these terrible unknown quantities, because you know only a handful of men—only a few— can do the job and you're proud to be one of the few. And when I found that out about George it made it easier somehow for me to work right at the same plant, with the same memories he had known, and I'm glad now that I decided to come back to Los Angeles."

"I admire you for it," said Judson. "I always wondered why you came back."

"I know I'm sounding speechy," she said, "but—"

"Could I have another drink?" he said. He knew he was being rude but he felt a sudden compulsion not to let her talk because he knew what she was going to say and he didn't want to hear it.

"Of course." She rose from her chair. "There's another thing I've found out, something I think is important."

"Excuse me," said Judson, "but I've got to talk to Lansdale."

But when he reached the doorway, he turned around and faced her. "I know what you're thinking. I think I even know what else you're going to say. But there's one thing you've left out. After a while, a man just goes to pieces, that's all. Something goes wrong here—"

He held up his unsteady hands, turning them over, palms up, then palms down.

"And then something goes wrong here—" He pointed to his temple. "And that's it. When that happens, a pilot's through. I've seen it happen to dozens of them. And I know what the doctors call it because I've seen them hang the tab on fifty men and then ground them."

He strode over to the blonde birch bookcase which held George's engineering textbooks. His fingers ran along the titles until he came to a volume that he knew well. George-town and Croxton's *Aeronautical Dictionary*.

Pulling it from the bookcase, he opened to the reference section and skimmed the definitions until he came to the one he wanted. *Aeroneurosis: A chronic functional nervous disorder occurring in professional aviators, characterized by gastric distress, nervous irritability. Often includes hallucinations, fear of flying.*

"Here—" He handed the book to Marjorie, his finger marking the place. "Read this and you'll find out what I'm talking about. And you'll see why I'm not flying the X-14A tomorrow!"

He went into the bedroom, dialed the Statler and swore when he received the same message. Lansdale was still speaking and could not come to the phone.

He sat down on the bed and did not look up as Marjorie came in, holding the book.

"Let me tell you something else," she said. "I've found out that a flier who won't fly is no good to himself or those around him. Tell me honestly, Jud, can you see yourself strapped to a desk in your father's canning plant for the rest of your life?"

"Of course not," he said. "The thought of it makes me sick."

141

"Then hear me out, Jud," she said.

The bedsprings moved slightly as she sat down beside him.

"Look at me, Jud," she said. "Look at me and understand me."

Her fingertips, cool and gentle, touched his chin and turned his face until they were looking at one another. With her other hand, she brushed a fallen strand of yellow hair from her cheek and he saw the fine texture of her skin and was struck by the intensity in her dark blue eyes.

"Jud," she said. "I want you to know now that I love you ... love you very much."

He moved, taken unawares, and she added: "No, don't interrupt me, Jud, please. I guess I first suspected I might be in love with you some months ago, but I didn't know for sure until the other night when you came here, into my bedroom and were so wonderfully good and gentle, so unlike what I'd expected, so unlike anything I'd ever known. I—"

He tried to speak but she laid her finger across his lips.

"I guess, Jud, that I love you even more than I loved George. In his own way, he was fine, but with you it's different. Being in love with you is bigger and more wonderful and more exciting and—" She paused and her voice dropped to a low, husky level. "And if anything ever happened to you, Jud, I couldn't stand it. I wouldn't want to live."

"Don't say that," he said, remembering Chally, "don't ever say that."

"But I must say it, Jud, because it's true. And that's why it tears me inside to tell you that you must fly the X-14A because in my heart I don't want you to take the risk. But in my mind I know you must, because if you don't fly that airplane tomorrow you'll hate yourself every day afterward that you live because you'll be living with a conscience that will give you no peace. That conscience will change you, it will ruin you and try to ruin those that are close to you, those that love you, like your father and Dunc—and me."

Judson got up from the bed. He drew out his pack of cigarettes and lit one, thinking about what she had said and not liking it.

"I know I've gone too far," said Marjorie. "I've said too much and you probably think I'm just another scheming

142

woman with her cap set for a man. It's not that way at all, Jud."

"I know it's not," he said.

He took her hands and drew her up from the bed. He kissed her gently on the lips.

"You're a hundred times the woman Chally was," he said. "I never healized it before. But I can't fly the X-14A, Marjorie. I can't."

"But you must," she said.

He drew away from her, went to the dressing table and ground the half-smoked cigarette angrily to dust in an ashtray.

"I want to—but I can't," he said. "My nerves are shot just like Bixler's were shot and I'm sure now, I can feel it, that it wasn't mechanical failure that made the YF-188 go in. It was Bixler's nerves and mine are just as bad. It's not that I'm afraid of dying. I got over that hurdle long ago. It's just that I'm afraid of smashing the X-14A and ruining Lansdale and the corporation and all the thousands of people that work for Lansdale."

He picked up the telephone and began dialing the Statler again.

"Please, Jud." Marjorie put her hand on his arm. "Don't call him."

"I've got to!" he said.

"Please, Jud!"

He kept dialing and he spoke through clenched teeth, his voice harsh and bitter. "I can't fly it—that's all there is to it! I haven't got the guts! I can't get in that cockpit and—"

She slapped him. He felt her fingers crack hard across his mouth and cheek and he was stunned, not from the minor pain of the blow, but stunned that she could do such a thing to him.

"I'm sorry, Jud. . . ."

Her face was suddenly very white and her lips quivered.

"I had to do it," she said, "because I know you *can* fly that airplane tomorrow, that you *can* do all that you must do up there and land it safely. You're the best test pilot in this country, Jud—the men at the plant have told me it again and again and I believe them. You're afraid and you have every right to be afraid. But I read your definition of aeroneurosis

143

and I don't think it applies to you and now will you hang up that phone and let me tell you why?"

Slowly he put the telephone back on its black cradle.

"Tell me," he said.

"You'll think I'm cruel," she said, "but I don't care. The thing that affected your flying was Chally and the fact that she wouldn't love you the way a wife should love her husband. And tonight when you found her dead you thought that was the end of your nerves—you thought you heard them snap and shatter."

She held his arm tightly and looked up at him and there were tears bright in her lashes.

"But you're wrong, Jud, you're wrong! Don't you see how she robbed you of your confidence? Don't you see how she filled you with doubts? She was unhappy and confused and I feel sorry for her, but she was also selfish and evil and she knew it when she married you. But she's gone now. And don't you see what it means, Jud? It means you've been purged!"

She continued to look up at him. Then she released her grip on his arm, turned and walked from the room.

For a time, he stood there, his hands opening and closing into fists at his sides, shocked by her words, shocked to his core. He had never seen Chally that way. Never. Even when he'd read her note and realized the implication of those hastily-written, scratched-out words.

He went out to the living room and sat down on the divan.

"You may be right," he said after a while.

"I said too much." Marjorie stood before the small, white-brick fireplace, winding an alarm clock. "Let's forget it all for now and get you to bed. What time will you have to get up?"

"I'm not sleepy," he said.

"Nevertheless you're going to bed," she said firmly, smiling. "Shall I set the clock for four-thirty?"

"You seem pretty sure I'm going to do it," he said.

"I hope you don't think I'm too pushy, Jud, Do you?"

"No," he said, "because I guess you're right. I guess I'll have to do the best I can tomorrow."

"Good," she said, "Now you get in there and get undressed and I'll bring you something warm to drink."

She went toward the kitchen, not looking back at him, and he could tell that she was deliberately trying to underplay the importance of what he had said, and he was glad she had chosen to do it that way because it made it easier.

Returning to the bedroom, he peeled off his clothes and got into bed. In a few minutes, Marjorie came in with a glass of warm milk and a sleeping pill. As he swallowed the small white oblong, he thought of Chally and he felt the tension again in his thigh muscles and the sickness in his stomach and he could drink only half the milk.

"Drink it all," she coaxed.

"Milk," he grimaced. "Tastes like hell."

But he managed to drink the rest of it.

"I know it was a hard decision to make." Marjorie took the glass from him and set it on the night stand. "But important decisions are never easy. It must have been very hard for all of them, men like the Wright brothers and Langley and Lindbergh, on the night before they made their flights."

"Christ," he said, "don't go putting me in their class."

"But you are in their class, Jud. Won't you be flying faster tomorrow than any one has ever flown before?"

He shrugged, trying to be casual and feeling the sleeping pill already starting to do its work. "I will if the wing stays in one piece."

"Shame on you," she smiled.

She tucked the pink woolen blanket in around his feet and took the glass from the night stand.

"Can I ask you something, Jud?"

He closed his eyes. "Sure."

"Can I go with you tomorrow—to Edwards?"

He nodded, feeling a pleasant drowsiness which soothed and warmed his muscles. "If you want to. But why do you want to?"

"Because I want to be there and pray for you, darling. . . ."

"What did you say?" He wanted to open his eyes and look at her but he was too sleepy.

"I want to pray for you," she said.

"Didn't you say something else?"

"Darling?" she said.

"That's what I thought . . . you said." He was too drowsy to make his words clear. "And I . . . like it."

Very easily, like falling and falling through space, he went to sleep.

145

Chapter Twenty

HE AWOKE in the dark half an hour before the alarm was supposed to go off, sweat covering his body, the fragments of a nameless nightmare departing so quickly from the drugged corridors of his brain that he could not remember what it had all been about. He sat on the edge of the bed until his head cleared and then he put on his slacks and groped his way through the gloomy house to the kitchen.

When Marjorie came out, he was drinking his first cup of hot coffee, holding the cup tightly so she could not see his fingers trembling.

"Something wrong?" she asked anxiously. "Couldn't you sleep?"

"Slept like I'd been clubbed," he said. "And I've been thinking. I'd like Dunc to come along, too. Won't hurt him to miss one day of school."

"Wonderful," she said. "He'll love it!"

He shaved, finished dressing and refused her offer of bacon and eggs because his stomach still didn't feel right. He drank two more cups of coffee and they left the house at quarter to five, Marjorie wearing a trim yellow blouse and a cinnamon-colored suit.

They drove in the Jaguar to Judson's house and the gray misty light of early morning was breaking as he went quietly up the staircase and along the hall to Dunc's bedroom. He touched the boy's arm and awoke him, whispering a quick explanation in the small ear and cautioning him to be quiet so they would not awaken their father.

"Jeepers!" whispered Dunc. "You're really going to let me see you fly one? No fooling?"

"No fooling," said Judson.

As he watched Dunc scramble into his jeans and T-shirt, his young eyes aglow with anticipation, he knew he was doing the right thing. Even if something should happen, even if the wing should fail, it was right for the boy to be there.

When they got to the plant, they were in time to board the first shuttle Navion. Judson and Marjorie sat in the back, letting Dunc enjoy the important seat up front next to the pilot where he could watch the instruments, look out the window and ask questions to his heart's desire.

It was a quick trip, too quick to satisfy Judson, and when they touched down at the main base at Edwards he could feel the sweat under his shirt even before they stepped out onto the asphalt under the warm rays of the rising desert sun.

He had no difficulty getting Marjorie and Dunc through the first security gates, but the Air Police balked at the final gate until Lansdale himself, who was standing near the tail of the B-29, noticed and came over. A word from him and they were admitted.

Lansdale drew Judson aside and then halted beside the B-29 as Marjorie and Dunc went on ahead to the spectator's section. Judson glanced up at the X-14A, noting that it was locked securely to the bomber's belly, fuel aboard and ready to go.

"I want to talk to you a minute," said Lansdale.

"Something wrong?" said Judson, half hoping the X-14A wasn't ready and that the flight was being delayed.

Lansdale shook his head. "Everything's set. It's just that I'm concerned about what happened to your wife, Jud, and I want you to know how sorry I am."

"Thanks," said Judson. He couldn't think of anything else to say.

"General Eberle heard about it, too," said Lansdale, "and he doesn't think you should do the test. He thinks it would be too tough on your nerves, too much to ask. He says he's got a young Major who's hot as a pistol and ready to do the test instead."

Lansdale paused and Judson, looking at him, thought the V-shaped scar on his chin looked whiter than it had on previous days.

"I'm leaving it up to you, Jud," he said. "Do you feel you can do it—or don't you?"

It was the opportunity Judson would have gone out of his

147

way to seek yesterday and for a moment, only a moment, he hesitated.

"I'm ready," he said. "About as ready as I'm ever going to be."

"Good boy!" Lansdale slapped him on the shoulder and they walked together toward Building L2 as the crew chiefs started the engines warming on the B-29.

In side the building, they crossed over to a section of metal lockers where an Air Force sergeant was waiting with Judson's T-1 pressure suit. Judson stripped off his slacks and the sergeant helped him into the clumsy olive-drab T-1, a far more complicated device than the G-suit he customarily wore for slower supersonic flight. The sergeant drew the corset-like laces on his arms and legs tight but not tight enough to shut off his circulation.

"Well, Jud," said Lansdale, "here's the ticket."

Reaching inside his coat, he got out the test card and handed it to Judson.

Judson scanned the penciled lines. *Climb to 95,000 feet or higher if practical. Left and right roll at Mach 3. Attempt higher speed if sufficient fuel left. Fuel Duration: 4 minutes.*

"Any questions?" asked Lansdale.

Judson shook his head.

"Did you do those cockpit check-offs like I suggested to familiarize yourself with the controls and procedures?"

"Yes," lied Judson because it would be useless to say no. Lansdale would want to know why and of course he couldn't tell him about the clanks.

"Good enough." Lansdale rubbed his eyes and Judson saw new lines of fatigue and weariness in the older man's face. "There's one other thing, Jud, I want to say before we go out there. I might be wrong about the wing and I want you to promise me something."

"Name it," said Judson.

"If anything happens," said Lansdale, "eject, understand? Don't try to be a god damn hero!" .

Judson nodded and they left Building L2 and walked back into the brightness and heat of the sun. The B-29's engines were ticking over and its crew and the additional rocketmen were aboard and waiting. Dozens of other men, some in uniform and some not, technicians, cameramen, engineers and

148

designers, were collected in clusters at respectful distances from the big bomber's blurring propellers.

Marjorie and Dunc saw him and came toward him through the crowd.

"Jeepers," said Dunc, looking at the T-1 suit, "you look like a man from Jupiter. How does it feel?"

"Tight," grinned Judson.

He turned and looked at Marjorie, saw the quiet confidence in her dark blue eyes and he was glad she was there.

She went up on tiptoe and kissed him lightly on the chin.

He squeezed her arm and then the sergeant helped him put on his helmet, fastening it so there would be an airtight seal where it joined the T-1 suit. Spallanzani and Haynes came up, shook hands and escorted him to the B-29. General Eberle and the Undersecretary of the Air Force, a small mustached man in a gray Homburg, shook hands just before he went up the ladder and he was reminded that this was how it had been just before Bixler took off. He remembered the dark burning streak of the YF-188 on the hard desert floor and he felt the fear twisting and turning in him again like a cold shapeless object from one of his nightmares. Then he went quickly up the metal rungs into the bomb bay, the door closed and in a moment the B-29 began to taxi.

With the ponderous thirteen-ton burden of the X-14A attached to its belly, the B-29 required nearly an hour to push its way into the stratosphere. The sky was cloudless but a hundred-mile-an-hour wind was blowing and the big bomber bumped along like a heavy truck on a rough road. The pilot told Judson they would be in position in ten minutes and Judson left the pilot's compartment, carrying his bailout bottle and oxygen hose, and walked back to the bomb bay.

Part of the X-14A's stainless steel fuselage protruded up into the bay like the smooth hump of a whale. One of the crewmen slid open the outer canopy and Judson climbed in, moving swiftly because of the restrictions of the T-1 suit, and sat down in the cockpit. He was annoyed by how small and cramped the cockpit was. There was hardly room enough to move his arms and legs freely. The crewman closed the outer canopy and Judson closed the inner canopy. He connected his

149

pressure and oxygen hoses, the headset line and his safety straps. Then he made certain the instruments and the four rocket switch on the simplified panel were positioned exactly as he remembered them from the blueprint specifications.

"Nearly there," the bomber pilot said over the inter-com.

"Roger," said Judson.

Despite the leather gloves, his hands were cold and he rubbed them together, scanning the test card in its clip on his knee, going over the procedures again and again in his mind, realizing that he was as scared as he had ever been in his life, wondering about the wing, feeling trapped like an animal in the tiny cockpit.

"We're at 20,000," announced the pilot.

It was the signal for the two rocket crewmen to swing into action. They waved at Judson and started topping his tanks with the dangerously volatile "lox," liquid oxygen.

Judson checked his watch and called over the inter-com to the bomber pilot: "Switch off B-29 power!"

"Power off!" said the pilot.

A glance at his instruments showed Judson that the power from the bomber's electrical system had been switched over to the X-14A's.

"I've got power," he told the pilot.

"Roger," came the answer. "One minute to drop!"

Judson tried to swallow, but his mouth was too dry. He flipped a switch, noting that the B-29's speed was a slow 204 knots.

"Lox prime on," he said.

He waited for the crewmen to check their section and then came the curt reply: "Lox prime showing" and he knew she was just about lit.

He squirmed in the seat wishing the pilot would start his count and then finally the voice, taut and strained, came over the inter-com: "Five . . . four . . . three . . . two . . . one . . . DROP!"

Released from the mother ship, the X-14A floated easily down out of the bomb bay, barely flying. Judson shoved the nose down into a dive to pick up speed and then from the edge of his eye he saw the observer F-160K flying chase beside him, not more than a couple of hundred yards away.

Judson threw the first switch and called: "Firing One!"

Almost immediately the observer F-160K called back: "Rocket One Firing!"

Judson got the nose up and in quick succession he fired Rockets Two, Three and Four, feeling the tremendous fear in his belly, marveling at the way his gloved fingers were doing what they were supposed to be doing.

"Two, Three and Four firing!" called the observer pilot, already falling far behind.

After that there was no time to be afraid; he was too busy.

The heavy airplane went up in a steep climb, almost straight up, knifing effortlessly through the upper-air turbulences, and though he had known it would be like this he was astonished at the unlimited power of the rockets. The tremendous acceleration kept him pinned against the backrest, but she handled well, pushing her needle nose up into the stratosphere at an ever-increasing velocity. Judson watched the hands on the altimeter move steadily to 40,000, to 50,000, to 60,000, to 70,000 feet, saw that the four rocket pressure indicators were normal, saw the machmeter indicator touch 1.2. It was incredible. *Faster than the speed of sound and still in a steep climb.*

Up, up, up and further up. Faster.

He checked his watch. He'd been climbing for nearly two minutes and that meant nearly half his fuel was gone. It was time to start leveling out to test the wing in the supersonic rolls.

Gently he eased forward on the stick, set the trim and watched the nose slowly drop back to the horizon. The altimeter read 101,000 feet and he was surprised at how quickly he had picked up those other 30,000. As he entered the pushover into level flight, his whole body felt light, weightless because of the forces at work, and suddenly the test card, which had become loosened in its clip, floated up into the cockpit and hung suspended for a moment.

He completed the leveling out curve and the X-14A, relieved of the task of climbing, became a thing unleashed. He permitted himself a split second to look down, to see what the earth looked like from 101,000 feet, saw the desert curving away deep into Mexico, saw Arizona and saw the snowy reaches of Northern California's mountains. But there was no

151

more time for sightseeing. The X-14A's speed was approaching the fantastic. Mach 2, twice the speed of sound, and then Mach 2.2 and 2.5 and 2.8.

There was supersonic yaw, with the airplane easing slightly to left and right, but nothing that couldn't be corrected with slight pressure on the controls. Faster and faster and then he was at Mach 3 and it was time for the rolls and he knew that if the wing were going to break the rolls would do it. He put in right aileron and around she went, turning well despite the great forces. Then left aileron and she rolled left. He felt a thrill of accomplishment and even though everything was being recorded on the research gear he wanted to let them know downstairs that he'd done it.

He tripped the mike button. "Rolled at Mach 3. Satisfactory."

"Good," came Gadford's voice from the flight tower. "How much fuel left?"

"Thirty seconds," he said.

"Easy does it," said Gadford.

"Roger," said Judson.

He watched the machmeter needle move to 3.3 and, feeling the sweat on his shirt and the warmth inside the T-1 suit, he suddenly wished it was over with. Swiftly the needle swept to 3.5 and 3.6 and he heard the rockets begin to misfire and he knew he was getting close to the end of the line. He felt himself growing warmer—or was he only imagining it? Or was the whole airplane in danger of burning up from the terrible friction of the air?

The needle went abruptly to Mach 4.02 and he knew he was traveling at least 3600 miles an hour in an absolutely unknown realm of speed, far far faster than the speed of a rifle bullet and he wished he could feel some other sensation besides his desire to get it over with. And then at last the long seconds were finished and the rockets, their three tons of fuel exhausted, sputtered and died.

The machmeter needle dropped quickly below 4 as the deceleration set in. Then quickly to 3.8 and to 3.7, too quickly, and he felt himself thrown forward hard against his safety straps. Harder and harder against the straps. He had never known such deceleration.

He fought to maintain control but the X-14A was suddenly a different airplane, a crazed creature that would not respond. She began to fall.

Chapter Twenty-one

EVERY PRESSURE he used on the stick and pedals was the wrong pressure. He swore because he had not expected such deceleration and wasn't prepared for it. The nose went down and nothing he did would bring it back up. He hung forward in his straps, feeling them cut deeply into his shoulders despite the thickness of the T-1 suit, and then the airplane was wobbling in a completely uncontrolled plunge.

He was sure at first that he could bring her out of it as soon as she slowed sufficiently. She hurtled downward but then abruptly her motion changed and she was tumbling, tail first and then nose first, tumbling at tremendous super speeds, the razor thin wing and stabilizer getting no grip on the thin, rarefied air, tumbling like a leaf in a great void.

Thrown against his straps, slammed back against the seat, Judson yelled in the terror of it. Once as his head rocked on his shoulders he caught a glimpse of the altimeter and saw that he had fallen to 70,000 and he knew he had to get out while there was still time before the airplane tore itself to pieces.

He tried to slide his hand along the armrest to the ejection lever that would jettison the cockpit. His hand would not move. He did not know which way the airplane was falling now; all he knew was that the forces of the fall were so great every muscle was immobilized. He screamed deep in his throat, the sound reverberating inside his helmet, and again tried to move his hand those seven inches to the ejection lever. His fingers could not budge.

Tumbling, tumbling. And then for a blessed few moments she steadied, her nose aiming straight down, and he thought

153

he felt control under the hand that was on the stick. He moved the stick slightly and then he lost all control once more and he felt her begin to tuck as the dive became more inverted and went over on her back.

As he hung there, upside down, the pressures of the inversion threw him against his straps until he thought they would burst. A pink haze settled before his eyes and he felt the pressures in the T-1 suit fail to combat the force that was cramming the blood from his body into his brain. The pink haze turned pinker, then redder, blood red, and he felt his cheeks swelling outward and felt his eye-balls protruding and felt a pain in his head that was like a hot red flame and he knew this was it, this was red-out. He thought of Marjorie suddenly, Marjorie and not Chally, and thought desperately how he wanted to be with her and then there was a final exploding pressure behind his eyes and he redded out into unconsciousness.

It seemed that a long interval passed before he was aware again that he was still falling. He tasted blood in his mouth and as his eyes focused he found himself slumped against the right console because his right shoulder strap had broken. The X-14A was spinning slowly, still inverted, and his eyes sought the instruments and saw that he was at 22,000 feet, moving at Mach 1.2. His brain functioned laboriously and he could not believe that the airplane was still intact. When he moved his head, he felt an intense pain in his neck. Slowly he looked out and saw that the wing was still there and then, moving ponderously like an automaton, he neutralized the controls. He applied hard opposite rudder, as hard as he had strength for, and the airplane began to recover. He was so tired he did not really care whether he got her out of it or not. She came up slowly, the nose lifting, and he let her find her own way, keeping just enough control so she would not stall.

He heard voices in the headset and knew they were worried frantic by now wondering what had happened, but he did not want to waste the energy that would be required to reply. He slumped back against the seat, barely keeping his head up because of the pain in his neck. He saw shattered bits of plastic glittering in his lap and he wondered where they had come from. The F-160K chase plane came up on his right wing and the pilot called to him on the radio asking if he was all right but he did not feel like replying.

Powerless, the X-14A glided at a swift downward angle. He saw the long main runway and decided he was going to line up pretty well. He knew he was balancing on the thin rim of consciousness and that any sudden reaction could put him under. His final approach was not clean. There were no flaps to cut his speed and even after he got the wheels down the additional drag did not slow him sufficiently. The runway came up fast, extremely fast, and the tires shrieked as they hit hard at 220 knots. She bounced high and he thought he'd lost her but she settled back to the runway again and he remembered vaguely, seeing the instrumeints through haze, that the para-brake handle was there somewhere. When he pulled it and the chute billowed out from the tail, slowing her down, he was thrown hard forward, hitting his shoulder on the console because of the broken strap, and he was powerless to keep himself from sliding into unconsciousness again.

He sagged against the console, not seeing anything but keeping his hand on the stick, and through the blackness he felt her leave the runway and begin to roll over the hard-packed floor of the dry lake. She rolled for a long time but he didn't know how long or how far.

It was quite a while before they got to him. He heard someone speak.

"Judson, can you hear me?"

He looked around slowly, feeling the pain in his neck, and saw that they'd gotten the plastic canopies partway open. He noticed that the inner canopy had a shattered, spider-web ·dent where his helmet had struck it during the fall. An Air Force ambulance was parked alongside and he realized the voice he'd heard was that of a young flight surgeon standing on a ladder which had been placed against the airplane's flank.

"Can you get out?" asked the flight surgeon.

Judson tried but he couldn't make it and they helped him, lifting him gently from the cockpit and carrying him down the ladder. Another ambulance arrived, followed by a fire truck and a blue staff car whose doors flew open before it halted and Lansdale and General Eberle got out. In the small throng that was forming, Judson looked for Marjorie because there were so many things he wanted to tell her and

155

then he saw her, arriving in a second staff car with Dunc and some officers.

Despite his protests that he was all right, they placed him in a stretcher, got his helmet off and the flight surgeon's fingers tenderly explored the skin area around his neck.

And then finally Marjorie was kneeling beside him and Dunc was there with his small face shining and Marjorie's tear-warm cheek was wet against his cheek and he didn't care what the others might think about him embracing another woman so soon after what had happened to Chally.

"I knew you could do it, darling!" Marjorie said. "I just knew you could!"

"But not without you," he said. "You were there with me all the way. I—"

There was no more chance for them to talk then because Lansdale had shouldered his way up to them, followed by General Eberle and the Undersecretary of the Air Force. Lansdale's face was pale and slick with sweat.

"Jud!" he said. "Are you okay?"

"He's all right," replied the flight surgeon. "Neck ligaments are sprained but he's all right."

"Thank God!" Lansdale seized Judson's hand and pumped it furiously. "Congratulations, Jud! I don't know how you did it!"

The Undersecretary stepped closer and shook his hand and so did General Eberle.

"A marvelous accomplishment," said the Undersecretary. "We're proud of you!"

"But what happened up there?" said Lansdale. "We nearly all went crazy!"

"Deceleration," said Judson. "I wasn't prepared for it."

"Was it the wing?" demanded Lansdale. "Something wrong with the wing?"

"There was nothing wrong with the wing," said Judson. "It operated at Mach 4.02 with minimum turbulence."

"Mach 4.02!" said Lansdale. And then he repeated the words as if he couldn't believe them. "Mach 4.02?"

Judson nodded. "She's a lot of airplane. She rolled clean and then stayed intact in an 80,000-foot tumble."

"Mother of God!" said Lansdale slowly.

For a moment, no one said anything.

Then two of the attendants picked up the stretcher and started toward the first ambulance.

"Would you fellows turn me around a second?" said Judson.

They did as he asked and he looked at the X-14A, looked at the long, beautiful, stainless steel lines of her and it felt tremendously good not to be afraid of her any longer. She had done her worst and he had been equal to her with his hands firm on the controls. He thought about the tests to come, those to solve the deceleration problem and then Mach 5 and Mach 6 and even faster, and he felt a great pride that he would be the one to do them.

"Okay," he said to the attendants. "Let's go."

END